K.M. Robinson
MULAN
DRAGON SHIFTER

MULAN DRAGON SHIFTER
Copyright © 2020 by K.M. Robinson.

Published by Crescent Sea Publishing.
www.crescentseapublishing.com

Cover designed by Cover A Day.
www.coveraday.com

To Tiffy, who introduced me to one of my new favorite types of storytelling...this book is all your fault.

Chapter 1

A PIERCING SCREECH FILLS THE VALLEY. GLASS IN the windowpanes rattle as the mighty beast goes by, flapping its wings. It dips low over the town, forcing air to barrel through the streets, knocking people off balance.

"I have to go. I'm so sorry, Mulan."

"Keung, wait!" I shouldn't have called to him—I know better—but I couldn't help myself. "You're not ready to go back."

Stepping toward me, Keung takes my shoulders in his hands. "It's been two months since you found me, Mulan. You healed me."

Keung cups my chin in his hand as he tilts my gaze up to meet his. The lieutenant's kiss is soft, piercing my very soul. My hand snakes out from my side, wrapping around his waist and I will us back to the blanket we laid on yesterday, eating lunch in the sparkling afternoon sun outside of the hospital where he had been staying to recover.

He obliges as I pull him closer, running his hands through my hair. Everything sparks under his touch. The bottom of his long hair tickles my wrists as my hands brush over the back of his belt in my foolish attempt to keep him by my side.

"I have to go," he shouts, pulling away quickly as another dragon flies overhead, screaming commands at the army. "I'll come back to you, Lin Mulan. When the war is over, I'll come back to you."

Smirking over his shoulder, he blows a kiss at me. The moment he turns away, he shifts. Red wings lift him into the sky over the pointed and sloped buildings; he's careful not to cause too much of a wind tunnel as he takes flight, sparing the merchants' tables and wares.

I lower my hand from where it had been outstretched to him. Two months wasn't enough time. His wounds from the battle had healed but I wasn't ready to say goodbye.

"They're calling for a conscription!" A woman's voice rises above the noise of the vendors and floats to the alley Keung and I were hiding in to say goodbye. "They demand our men to go to war!"

There wasn't supposed to be a conscription—the enlisted men are to meet in the Center, but now we have to send our sons to war with them? Chen's army must be escaping us with the black jade blossom—we can't let that happen.

"It is an honor to serve the emperor and the province, woman!" a man shouts in return.

"They would take our sons!" she fires back as I round the corner, hurrying to see what is happening. "Every family must provide a warrior to join the army *today*. They don't even have time to prepare!"

Her screams turn to hysterics as she clutches a toddler in her arms. The merchants try to calm her, but the women in the crowd pick up her cries.

Suddenly, as if realizing it all at the same time, the crowd disperses, rushing to their homes. If what the woman says is true, we'll all have to provide a dragon to fight in the emperor's army to fight to get our life source back.

"Jinhai," I whisper. My brother will be forced to fight. His dragon scales will protect him from attack, but he'll die anyway, and it will be my fault.

I race through the town past ancient, angled buildings and pagodas, knocking into people running for their homes. Ripples of whispers fill the streets, "It is an honor."

An honor. How is it an honor to burn cities and die for the province? It is a necessity, but there's only obligation, no honor.

Yet, I know giving oneself to protect others is the most valiant and selfless thing a person can do, which is why I know my brother will never survive this war.

"Mulan!" Father's voice is strong as I crash into the house. "Steady, child."

Ancient-looking paintings fill the walls of the house as screens block off sections of the main room. A cluster of lanterns hangs in one corner, their tassels reaching halfway down the wall. The short table on the far side of the room is covered with a project my little sister was working on, but she's nowhere in sight.

"Where is Jinhai?" I demand, forgetting all about my teary goodbye with the lieutenant moments ago. My gaze darts around the house searching for him.

Painted fans on the wall flash in my sight as I search. Bowls with luxurious markings resting on shelves blur in my vision. I filter out the soft music coming from the other room.

"What's going on?" Father orders information. As a retired general for the army, he knows how to get us to tell him things. Despite his injury, he is still terrifying.

"The army needs men, Father." Jinhai steps into the

house, closing the door behind him. I step out of his way. "A dragon is required of each family."

"I'll go," Father proclaims.

"No!" my twin and I banish the thought at once.

"I'll go, Father," my twin announces.

"You can't," I protest. "You'll die."

"I'm not as strong as I should be, Mulan, but I'm not a lost cause." Jinhai glares at me. *I'm to blame.*

The door bangs open, knocking objects off a shelf. Mother stands in the light, a force scarier than Father.

"Kuo." Her voice is chilling.

"I know, my love." Father walks to her, wrapping an arm around her shoulders. "He will be fine. He is ready."

Mother shrugs him off and walks to Jinhai's side. "You are strong, my boy. You will serve the province well. You'll remain in the area for a few days, so we don't need to pack you yet, but you're due in the Center within the hour. You should go *now*. Get dressed."

"He can wait a *few* minutes, Mother." Ming peeks out of her room. "It won't take an hour to get to the Center."

"Your brother will be early, Ming. It shows strength and preparedness. He will find favor with the generals."

I wonder if he'll be serving with the lieutenant now. Perhaps he'll be in the Center when I take Jinhai to drop him off.

"He will find favor with the generals because of Father," Ming replies, unafraid of Mother's reaction. Mother's jaw tightens but she chooses not to argue when she could be putting her energy into preparing her son for battle.

Jinhai slips away to get ready, holding eye contact with me for a moment as he scoots around the furniture and green plants mother keeps in the house.

"Your brother will find favor for many reasons, Ming. He is a fearsome dragon from a strong family line. He will be fine in battle and will return to us victorious with the rebels' heads on pikes."

Ming's eyes grow wide.

"Jinhai will be fine, Ming. He'll do his duty and make our family proud, and we will keep things safe at home for him, won't we?" I jump in. Ming is far too young to talk about the horrors of the war. "Now, Jinhai has to go get his orders. I'll take him there and make sure he doesn't get lost on his way home tonight. Why don't you and mother make his favorite dish for dinner so we can send him off properly?"

Ming rushes to Jinhai as he reappears dressed to go and wraps her arms around his waist. "See you tonight."

I jerk my head toward the door, knowing my twin needs an escape. The room suddenly feels overly warm.

"See you tonight." He tears himself away, waving to Mother without looking and follows me out the door.

"That was intense," he comments.

"Let *me* go," I beg him quietly. This should be *my* duty.

"No." His tone is harsh. Balling his fists by his side, he quickens our pace, trying not to let his face reflect his frustration.

"They said dragons," I push, "not sons."

"You can't be a dragon in Yan Liu, Mulan. I will go."

We turn the corner, moving faster. He's going to shift soon; I need to watch so I don't fall behind.

"But—"

"No, Mulan!" Jinhai halts. My shoulder slams into him. So much for watching closely. "You will not go to war. I won't allow it. And they won't accept you anyway."

"Jinhai—"

My head snaps back as he grabs my shoulders and shakes me. His eyes burn intently into me with such ferocity that I step back. He keeps his grip on me.

"I may not be as powerful as the others, Mulan, but I am trained well. I've been compensating this entire time, and no one has ever guessed. I'll be fine."

I'm terrified for him, but I don't dare say it.

"I'll be fine, Mulan." He softens his words. "You don't need to worry about me.

"Besides," he says, smirking, "shouldn't you be more worried about your *lover*?"

My eyes grow so wide they should fall out of my head. "*How—?*"

"How did I know you were lusting after that lieutenant you found out in the woods and brought back to the hospital? I'm not blind, sis."

"I made sure I wasn't followed." *How did he see me?*

"I was in town and saw you." He pauses. "Don't worry, I wasn't snooping. You shouldn't be so obvious about your love, Mulan."

"It's been two months; it's not love," I protest, looking away.

His hands slide down my arms to clasp my hands. My brother shakes them playfully. "Don't worry, I'll keep an eye on your *beloved* while we're at war. I'll probably be working under his command anyway." A terrifying thought.

"Maybe he'll get roughed up a little bit—he's too pretty for you."

Seeing my opportunity, I take it. "I've seen his scars, Jinhai. He's plenty roughed up. *You* just can't see them when he's fully dressed."

Jinhai pales, nearly dropping my hands. "It's a good thing I know you only mean in the hospital while you were caring for him, or I'd have to kill my commanding officer."

"You know I'd—"

He taps my nose, cutting me off. "You're far too meek for that, Mulan. Now, let's move along."

My brother turns, stepping away from me so he can shift. I follow suit and transform into my dragon form, careful not to be seen, and lift away from the town. Buildings grow small as we take to the air. The wind is cool against my scales, but I don't mind. Few like me get to have this experience, so I remind myself to revel in it while I can.

Jinhai looks back at me, eyes gleaming. I watch for a moment as he dips, his blue scales shining against the bright sun. I've always been jealous of his shading—it's my favorite color. Or, perhaps it's my favorite because it is my brother's coloring. My jade scales just aren't as appealing.

I tip, following Jinhai as he veers off course, directing us to an area just outside of the Center where I won't be noticed transforming back into a girl. When we land, we'll walk to the Center together, able to speak again.

Small children run in the colorful streets below. Not too long ago, I was one of them. Now I've grown and become a tea leaf merchant like my parents. I resist the urge to flap my wings extra hard as we glide over one of our competitors—a man who actively works to steal our customers with his inferior products.

Jinhai dips, diving low suddenly. He twirls around to watch my reaction. This is a game to him...as if he weren't about to go off to war unprepared, despite his years of training to defend the village if need be.

I ignore him, staying on track. If I give into his playfulness, we'll end up late and Mother would have my hide long after Jinhai disappears from our lives to serve the province. Jinhai snorts disapprovingly but returns to my side.

Ahead, other dragons make their way to the Center to report to their new commanders. Bright colors fill the air as they fly in, landing in the distance and transforming.

After a few minutes, Jinhai dives low, looking for a clear space to land. I slow my flight, waiting for him to make his choice. Behind a line of buildings and trees, he dips down.

When my feet touch the ground, I transform as quickly as possible, darting for the bushes to avoid being noticed should we have overlooked any bystanders. When I emerge, my twin is waiting.

"Didn't feel like racing today?" He crosses his arms teasingly.

"Not when Mother would skin me alive for making you late, brother." I reach up and tuck the hairpin back into my long bangs to hold them out of my face. "Now, before we go, let's make you presentable."

He turns, allowing me to run my fingers through the length of his hair and tie it low down on his back after braiding a small section of it. He adjusts his collar and spins for me to see.

"How is it that your transformations never mess up your hair, Mulan?"

"Benefits of Mother's line," I reply. "You have more of Father in you, and boys aren't so lucky."

"Are you saying the matriarchal line is superior?" he taunts, starting to walk toward the Center, arms still crossed over his chest. It's a good look for him—one he'll need on the battlefield. "If that's what you're saying, then we have no hope of surviving this war."

His serious note hits me like a punch to the gut in training and races through my body like ice. I am my Mother's daughter, but he didn't get her strength—I took that from him. The men walking into this war have the blood of the province in their veins, not that of the dragon I carry. Should anyone admit it, our enemies are indeed stronger, which is why we have to be smarter with our attacks. It's why my parents should allow me to go—at least I hold some hope against the enemy.

The province would never allow it—they're too afraid of the enemy. My scales are a secret.

"I'm not saying that." I roll my eyes. "You'll be fine."

He glances over. "You're not acting like I'll be fine, Mulan."

"I wish you'd let me go," I grumble. "I could help."

"No." His words are harsh and angry. "You wish you could save me, but I don't need saving, Mulan. I have every bit of the strength the rest of those men have. Just because you're one of the only girls in the province who can shift doesn't mean you're superior."

He doesn't, though—my brother isn't as strong as the other dragons and he knows it. I was never meant to be able to shift, but my mother's bloodline changed things for my family.

Jinhai has worked hard to keep up with the others, but I can always tell when he struggles—something I picked up from our training together. At least I was allowed to participate in that openly.

"You're not coming, Mulan. When we get there, go see your broken-lieutenant and then go home. I'll be back tonight to prepare."

Jinhai stalks off angrily ahead of me but ensures he doesn't get more than a few paces away. Only minutes older than me, he's convinced he has to care for me. Admittedly, he did when we were young, but not any longer. I suppose neither of us will give up our drive to protect the other.

"Jinhai!" voices shout as we walk into the Center. He raises his hands and laughs as if we hadn't just been fighting. Waiting, he loops his arm around my shoulders and pulls me in—something he likes to do to remind the boys that I'm off-limits to them.

"Mulan, nice to see you." They respectfully bow their heads to me. I nod back as they turn their attention back to my brother.

I don't get a step away before an explosion sounds in the Center and the ground ripples under my feet.

Chapter 2

"MULAN!" JINHAI SHOUTS, LUNGING AT ME TO PULL me down. I screech, forgetting I'm not in my dragon form. Hopefully the others assume it just sounded weird because I was being thrown to the ground.

"What was that?" I gasp, attempting to right myself from under my twin's heavy body. My shoulder hurts where he landed on me.

"Stay down," he hisses in my ear, pulling me to his chest to cover my head with his arms.

"Stop it, Jinhai." I struggle. "Let go of me."

The men around him leap to their feet, racing toward the scene of the explosion. I shove my brother to the side and stand before he can do anything else. Offering a hand, I wait to pull him up. He knows he only has two seconds before I walk away from him, so he takes my hand and follows. I've left him behind enough times that he knows if I need to investigate something, it's best to follow along because I won't wait or give up.

"Stay back, Mulan," Jinhai warns quietly, still holding my hand as I slow our run.

Fire crackles ahead as flames lick up poles and scorch the ground near what remains of the merchants' stands and carts on the outside of the Center proper. Murmurs race through the crowd and the voices of the commanders rise up to take control. They order men around to investigate.

"The enemy has been in our midst!" one leader proclaims.

I jerk up on my tiptoes when I see who is beside him —*my lieutenant*. He looks stern with his hands behind his back, feet apart, ready to fight any enemy that dares to come his way. Keung was so gentle with me when we spoke, but I've always been drawn to his fierce side. Even when I found him in that field in agony, he was a soldier prepared to fight, and only settled when he realized I wasn't a threat.

"Calm yourself, sister," Jinhai whispers. I can hear the laughter in his voice without even looking at his smirk. An elbow to the ribs shuts him up.

A third man races toward our leaders, leaning in to deliver information to the general. They both nod and Keung glances at them from the corner of his eye.

When the spy moves back, the general steps away from Keung and shifts, snapping into a fearsome-looking navy dragon. He takes to the skies without another word.

Keung looks into the crowd. "Today, the enemy has tried to stop us before your training even began. They came to our homes and tried to take us apart piece by piece. One of our lieutenants saw him and set off the explosion earlier than the man expected, killing them both, but sparing the lives of our men."

The crowd shifts, becoming agitated at Keung's words. I know what's coming—a rallying cry.

"We must act now, men! We will unite our training and take to the skies in one week's time! We will act swiftly and surprise Chen's army where they stand outside of the Zhao Wu Province they have stolen from their emperor!" He continues. Keung's words are compelling. Even the sisters and wives who accompanied their men to the Center seem eager to serve the province.

A young girl eagerly watches, relishing in the drama of the speech as she sways, eyes wide. She must be seeing someone off, though I can't tell who.

"Each family is to offer one dragon to serve for the province as we stop the tyranny of Chen's army and bring back the black jade blossom to save our province. We will not allow them to seize our life force and escape with it—condemning our province to a slow and painful death."

Keung pauses. "Dragons! Sign in here and receive your orders and postings. We begin at sunrise. Say goodbye to your families tonight—we move out as soon as our training is complete, but you will not see them again until we return from battle."

"I'll walk with you," I say, cutting off my brother's attempt at saying goodbye. He hurries to catch up with me as I walk away toward the tables. I give his name to the man behind the table before my brother can speak. "Lin Jinhai."

I shift forward on my toes as my twin nudges me to stop acting so aggressively. I elbow him back in response.

The man hands a rolled document to my brother with his assignments. I glance over it, looking for information about where he might be assigned.

"Mulan?" Keung's voice is soft behind me. His eyes grow wide as Jinhai and I both turn, realizing I'm not alone. He bows. "Lin Jinhai. Your sister spoke highly of you when tending to the sick in the hospital."

Jinhai eyes him. In any other situation, he would have had a retort, but he can't sass his commanding officer now that he has his orders. My brother tips his head back, acknowledging him with narrowed, squinting eyes meant to be the only threat he can offer Keung to stay away from me.

"Your sister was a great help to those of us in the army who—"

"Ah, so you know my lovely sister from the hospital," Jinhai interrupts him. "We're so proud of her many accomplishments."

"As you should be—" He stops as my brother cuts him off again, eyes widening in surprise.

"Yes, the matchmaker has high hopes for her. We're expecting an engagement any day now, though I suppose that will be delayed now with the war moving closer."

"Excuse me?" I whip around to face my brother—there is no matchmaker.

"Yes." Jinhai grins at the mortified look Keung is trying to suppress. "I'm sure it will be hard on her to wait, but at least she won't lose a husband to this war before she's even had time to be a wife to him. Anyway, pleasure to meet you, lieutenant. I'm sure I'll be seeing more of you. What was your name again?"

"Yu Keung," he mumbles in return as Jinhai brushes past him, pulling me along. I shake my head at Keung, praying he understands that it's not true.

A group of shouting men distracts my brother. He pulls me away before I can speak. Keung watches me go until I turn around to beat my twin.

"Jinhai!" I dig my nails into his arm until he releases me.

"Hey!" he shouts, turning to me as I punch his arm. "What was that for?"

"*Matchmaker?*" I scream. "There is no matchmaker, Father says I'm too young. What *was* that?"

"Eighteen is hardly too young to be married off, Mulan. Women wed far younger than that here. Father just doesn't trust anyone with you, and he certainly wouldn't trust that ladder-climber." What kind of research did he do on the lieutenant? "Yes, I know who he is, Mulan. Everyone knows who he is. The mountains may divide us, but his reputations proceed him."

Jinhai's jaw tightens as he speaks. He fights not to rush toward the men yelling a few feet away so he can finish his thoughts.

"I may not have recognized him when I saw you two together before, but I surely do now. Stay away from him and the others in this army, Mulan. If you think Mother will make you pay for making me late, you have no idea how much worse Father would do to me if he knew I allowed you in the presence of those men. Stay away from Yu Keung."

"But he—"

"No, Mulan!" Jinhai shouts. "If you're that desperate for love, marry Ning or Wei. They've always liked you, and I trust them more than I trust anyone from this army. Not that it matters, we're leaving in a few days."

"I don't want to get married," I protest, rushing after him as he turns his back and stomps away. "Keung is kind and gentle. He—"

My brother glares. He's never taken a stance like this before and it's terrifying.

"He's not what you think," I mumble. Summoning my courage, I add loudly. "Besides, as you said, you're leaving, so none of this even matters."

Jinhai watches me for a moment, lips pursed, before nodding once. The tension seems to roll off his neck and shoulders, bouncing to the ground as his eyes brighten and he offers a small smile.

"Come, let's see what the yelling is about and then we'll return for dinner and goodbyes."

Another explosion rocks the ground. We manage to stay on our feet this time, smoke rising several streets over.

More yelling ensues, as the soldiers and conscripted men rush toward the site.

"Rockets!" a man yells as a third explosion sounds. "They're going after the town!"

I look up just in time to see a small light in the distant sky. It arches, trailing down into the town in the direction we came from—Chen's men are going after the village. They must have meant to destroy the army at the same time as the villagers but that soldier caught the man early.

"To the skies!" one of the men shouts.

All around me, young men run, shifting as they move to get a head start on flight. They lift off, wings magnificently stretched out around them as they swiftly careen toward where Chen's men appear to be located.

"How did it become like this?" I whisper under my breath, running alongside my brother.

"Don't you dare," he hisses harshly. "Stay here and take care of the women."

Jinhai pushes me off course amidst the chaos. I can't be a dragon in front of these people—our women do not have these gifts—only the enemy does. There's no telling what might happen should I be viewed as an enemy in Yan Liu, especially given the recent attacks on the outer villages as Chen fights to escape with the black jade blossom.

Blue flashes in the corner off my eye as I peel off to give Jinhai space to transform. I rush toward a group of young girls huddled together. Light flashes toward us from the sky as the rocket drifts into our path.

"Move!" I scream, racing at them.

When I reach them, I pull them away from the pagoda, knowing Chen's men could have it ablaze within moments. I find the sturdiest building I can and leave them in the doorway with instructions to stay put. They call after me, but I can't stop—there are too many others that need help.

Lanterns sway each time an explosion sounds. The walls of buildings rattle. I push my family from my thoughts—Father will protect them, as will Mother should she need to unleash her scales. Ming will be safe with them.

In the sky, Jinhai races toward Chen's army, dodging rockets from the cannons below. Around him, dragons are shot from the sky.

I block out the people screaming around me, picking my way through the burning rubble of buildings that litter the streets. A small boy's sobs catch my attention and I come to an immediate halt.

Flailing, he dances around the street, clothing on fire. Too young to know what to do, his panic only seems to fuel the flames licking at his skin.

"I'm coming!" I scream, searching for water as I run.

A bucket catches my eye, miraculously still containing enough water to douse the boy's clothing and put out the fire. I can't hear whether or not he sizzles as I reach him with the liquid—the shattering screams in the air over-taking all of my senses at once.

A dragon screeches, plummeting from the sky. He crashes into the earth so hard, the ground rolls, and the rocks pile up like miniature mountains. In agony, he fights for his last breaths, clawing at the earth for more life but no one can help him. His wing burns, bent into the air at an odd angle. The poor dragon opens one eye to look for help, shuddering with each attempt at a breath. Blood leaks out from under him.

A woman screams next to me, jerking my shoulder around and ripping the toddler from my arms. He wraps his arms around her and sobs as she turns, taking her son somewhere safe.

Approaching a dying dragon is dangerous, but I only see the mercy in it. I'm slow, trying not to frighten him.

The dragon thrashes, his deep gray scales darkening with blood. His claws dig up the dirt, leaving wide ruts for me to avoid.

I kneel beside his head, putting my hand on his neck.

"Can you shift? Maybe I can help you."

The dragon moans, closing his eyes tightly. His body shakes with the effort, but he doesn't change form.

"Try again," I whisper. My heart breaks for him as pain seizes his body and he starts to convulse. I urge him to attempt to shift once more. "Try for me."

The transformation is slow, but successful, taking every breath the boy has. He rests in a pool of blood, clothing tattered from where he was injured—his human injuries are less severe than in his dragon form but still fatal. I gasp when I realize he's the neighbor boy down the street. He went to school with us as children. My mother even thought perhaps one day I would be matched with the boy—he was from a good family.

He groans as I look down at him. His eyes drift shut, and he's gone to meet the ancestors. I hold his head in my lap for another moment longer before honoring his sacrifice and leaving him behind.

I run toward the clearing outside of the Center where I can shift without being seen. The army has lost too many soldiers today. No one needs to know of my involvement, and with any luck, Jinhai won't catch me.

A familiar piercing shriek fills the sky. Overhead, my brother barely dodges a rocket. He darts forward, swooping low to go after Chen's men with the others.

I used my wings only a little while ago, but as I stretch them out, they feel like they haven't been free in dynasties. My ascent is slow and lumbering at first—I nearly crash into a tree as I rush to gain air—but once I make it over the tops of the branches, I'm free to fly however I please.

My vision darts from one side to the other, searching for where I can help. I'm far from the others which gives me the advantage of really looking at my surroundings.

The enemy army is small—only a portion of the legions of dragons Chen has at his command from the Zhao Wu and the provinces he captured and burned. He clearly doesn't intend to waste his armies destroying one that won't even officially exist until tomorrow.

Two dragons engage in a battle in the air. As I get closer, I have to dodge the dragons around me, looking for a target.

Jinhai will kill me when he finds out about this.

But not if that dragon racing toward him from the side kills him first.

Chapter 3

I can't let him die.

I won't let him die like this, a mere walking distance from our home before he even finished the paperwork to join the army.

Our parents will not suffer his loss and be left with only a tea peddler's daughters to care for them on their father's income alone. They need Jinhai more than they need me.

I angle myself toward the incoming dragon, prepared to force him out of the sky. His yellow scales make him easy to see as our army pushes back Chen's dragons in the air.

The collision is even worse than the shock of the rockets hitting the ground in the Center. We both move at odd angles, but I manage to right myself when he does not.

A second strike should take him out of the fight if I can land it correctly. Jinhai turns, noticing I'm there and shrieks at me—a warning, a threat? I don't know. I don't listen to him.

My cry is far more *terrifying* than *terrified*. The yellow dragon rights himself just as I scream again and race in his direction. I dodge a second dragon who thinks he can stop me, biting his lower neck so hard that blood rains down on the ground far below us.

Jinhai swoops in, destroying him as I turn to take on the yellow dragon. Everything goes quiet except the sound of my beating wings, each loud swooping sound serving to focus me more on my mission: end the yellow dragon....as if ending him would stop the entire war.

Whoosh.

Lower your head, Mulan.

Whoosh.

Prepare your feet, Mulan.

Whoosh.

Dig your claws in upon impact.

Take him down.

Whoosh.

Collide.

The yellow dragon falls after struggling to fight me. It's an easier victory than I thought. He takes out men on the ground who were too stupid to watch the world above them as they readied more cannons.

The onyx dragon going after Keung is much less naïve, though. I cry out in warning, but Keung has never seen me in dragon form and doesn't know the sound of my screech.

I lunge toward them. Jinhai cries out to me from behind. I can hear him coming after me, but I'm not going to let Keung fight this battle alone.

The dragon bites down on one of our soldiers before reaching Keung, plummeting the dragon down. He nearly hits the earth but pulls himself up and lands with more grace than I've seen any injured dragon land with before. He shifts to continue the battle.

My mind screams for Keung, willing him to hear my warning cries as I close in on them. I careen into the onyx dragon just as Keung turns.

I've never seen Keung in his dragon form close up—he's beautiful. The imperial army has never known a dragon more stunning. Markings cover his scales. The lieutenant opens his mouth to roar as I collide with our enemy.

I'm moving with such force that we don't stop until we crash into the ground, rolling over each other. Rocks pierce into my side and I'm suddenly quite thankful for my scales and the protection they offer.

In flashes as I roll, I see the dragons above us all turn to look, moving to attack us—I must be tumbling over their leader.

Our army uses the distraction to gain the upper hand and chase the dragons away. I come to a stop several steps from the edge of a cliff where we would have fallen to our fates while locked in a death grip.

Keung reaches us before Jinhai and the others do. I see him coming and flip so the onyx dragon is above me, leaving him wide open to be pushed by our lieutenant general. I suppose he rescued *me* as I rescued *him*, but I can't let Keung see me like this, and I won't be able to hide from him when he disposes of the dragon and turns back to me.

The moment Keung latches onto the dragon and rips him off me, I rush to the trees to shift, knowing it's my only chance. I hear the sound of the onyx dragon screaming in pain—his wing has nearly been ripped off his back as Keung tosses him over the edge mercilessly, a stark contrast to the gentleman I knew from the hospital the last two months.

The trees give me cover as I hurriedly transform. The injuries on my arms are minimal—I can explain them away if needed.

The leaves move around me as a tree collapses next to my human form. Spinning, I find Jinhai in dragon form glaring at me before jerking his head toward his back indicating I should climb on.

We're too far from the town to go back. I have no way of being here—no human could have run this distance on their own—so we'll need a story on why I'm so far from the Center and so close to the battle.

"What if we say I ran to help and ended up too far away. You saw me and brought me to protect me, but also because I could help the wounded?" I shout, climbing on his back. "Which I did, by the way."

He takes flight without answering me and I'm not sure if he heard my suggestion.

"Are you okay?" I call. Still, no reply.

I cling onto the spikes on his back as we float over the rocky cliffs and trees. The battle is dwindling. Below, I search for Keung, but he's already transformed below and is handling traitors alongside the general far from the cliff where I left him.

Jinhai looks for a safe place to land. Dragons settle everywhere, shifting to their human form to handle the dead and captives. We can't escape their gaze.

"Don't leave my side," my brother growls.

I'll pay dearly for my mistake of helping him.

As we approach, the leaders are shouting orders and demanding answers.

"I saw Lin Jinhai go in after him!" a man shouts, drawing our attention.

"Here he is!" shouts a man next to us. "Lin Jinhai, the general needs to see you."

Jinhai pauses a moment, fingers digging into my elbow—we've been caught.

I helped them—surely they should see I was protecting the lieutenant. They should know I'm not the enemy.

But only enemy women can fly—there are no dragon maidens in the Yan Liu province. This could mean my death or incarceration in some prison forever. This could mean my family's arrest and torture.

The crowd parts for us and Jinhai guides us through, fingers digging deeper into my arm as if he's trying to communicate to me.

He bows deeply, taking me down with him in front of Keung, the general, and the other officials. Terror courses through me, electrifying every inch of me. I can shift and fight if I must. If I can reach the village before the others, I can protect my family.

"Lin Jinhai, you saw the jade dragon that protected the lieutenant in battle, did you not?"

"Yes, general." Jinhai bows his head again.

"Where is he now?"

"I don't know, sir."

My eyes grow wide. Why doesn't he make up a lie? Say the dragon ran off. Say anything other than something vague.

I connect with Keung's gaze. It's wide with surprise. He looks like he wants to say something but turns back to the general.

"You followed him into the trees, did you not?" The general's voice is low and deep, far more terrifying than Keung's.

"Yes, sir."

"So, where is he? Everyone else has been accounted for. Who is this jade dragon? And who is *this*?" He adds, suddenly noticing me.

"My sister, general," Jinhai replies.

The general pauses, scrutinizing me. I'm the only one unaccounted for—apparently, he's going to figure it out.

The general's eyes grow wide, putting it together. He motions for them to seize me.

"The jade dragon is my twin, general!" Jinhai shouts. He's not lying.

The general freezes. I glance to his side, trying to get past the look of terror on Keung's face when he thought I was a traitor.

"It is my twin brother." Jinhai lies.

"You have a brother?" Keung questions. I've never

spoken of a brother to him other than Jinhai, and never by name.

"We're never seen together, general." My brother lies, dropping his voice conspiratorially. "My father was a great general in the emperor's army—Lin Kuo. He knew twin boys was an advantage. You will never see us together in human form, general. Not even *you* can order us to give up a secret advantage as great as that."

My brother is too bold. When we're discovered, we'll both die for this lie.

"Twins, you say?"

"Yes, sir. A tactical advantage to be in two places at once as no other man can do." He pauses. "Forgive us, we are under orders to proceed with this mission as planned without anyone knowing outside of this team."

"Fine." The general waves his hand dismissively. "We press forward. We chase their army and train along the way. We don't have time to go back now. Handle the girl."

If Jinhai is supposed to have a male twin who is the jade dragon, that means I can't leave. I now have a role to play, and if Mulan is sent home, the jade dragon disappears. I must figure out a way to stay with the army.

"General," I call. Jinhai pulls at me, silently begging me to stop speaking. "I can be useful as a medic, general. I'll come with you. There's no time to take me back, and it's too far for me to go alone, especially at this time of evening with Chen's men still in the area and the village potentially destroyed. Let me help your men."

He appraises me, looking me up and down.

"You will tend to their medical needs and stay out of their tents." He turns his back after his insult.

Jinhai's jaw drops as far as mine does at the insinuation, but not nearly as far as Keung's falls.

"The woman is off-limits," Keung finally shouts. "Do not disrespect your medic—she just may be the only thing saving your life, men. Move out!"

Hopefully the threat will keep lurkers away from me. Perhaps they'll allow me to sleep in my brother's tent during our travels for safety's sake, but I'll do as they ask. At least I'm not being beheaded for my scales.

My twin waits until everyone starts to walk away.

"Now what are we supposed to do?" he says angrily in my ear.

"At least they don't expect us to be seen together. I can shift for training and battles where they can't see me and no one will ever know."

"And what happens when the other medics realize you aren't helping the wounded?"

We follow quickly behind the masses. Twilight engulfs the mountains around us. Crickets chirp but I block them out.

"I'll run into the battlefield to help for the first few

minutes of the battles—they'll see me working. Soldiers can report my interactions with them. Then, I'll conveniently get lost in the trenches, working where the others aren't and no one will be the wiser when I shift and join you in the skies."

"I don't like this."

"You could have let me confess. Keung would have spared me."

Jinhai whips to face me. "No, he wouldn't have, and neither would the general."

He exhales sharply, then quietly asks, "Do you think they're okay?"

A lock of hair falls over my shoulder, brushing my cheek. Reaching up, I brush it away.

"Who?

"*Our family*, Mulan." He glances at me. "We just *left* the village to burn."

"Mother and Father will protect our people. They'll have no idea about us, though. Perhaps we can get a message to them."

"Perhaps you can fly back," he says pointedly.

"And leave you without a brother? No."

The group around us starts to shift. We'll pick up supplies at the next village before we move on.

"Guess you're riding," my brother says.

"I can go—"

"No, you can't. *Mulan* is now a part of the team and she can't fly. She has to get there somehow, so you're going to have to ride on my back when we travel and our *'brother'* can travel on his own without us."

"An efficient spy, isn't he?" I comment., smirking.

"Apparently he is. We'll have to figure out how to get some valuable information for him to give us later."

"Lan."

"What?" he asks.

We're the only two left on the ground—we're out of time.

"Our brother, Lan. After our ancestor." We're going to have to get our stories straight if we're going to pull his off.

"Very well." Jinhai looks up at the sky, taking stock off our now-depleted army. "Looks like you aren't the only woman after all."

He nods upward. In the sky, three other women sit on the backs of dragons.

"This will be interesting," I reply, climbing onto his back after he shifts.

Keung's red dragon form falls back, joining us for a moment before taking off higher into the sky. "Very interesting indeed."

When we land, the women and the general are waiting. None of them look happy.

Chapter 4

"You will remain with the woman, Daughter of Lin Kuo." The general brushes past me, leaving the women in his wake.

They bow their heads respectfully toward me.

"Your name?" the older woman asks. She can't be more than ten years older than me, but she carries the wisdom of our ancestors.

"Lin Mulan," my brother supplies. "My sister will be working with you, I see."

Behind us, the general starts barking commands. Glancing over my shoulder, I notice Keung at his side again, looking dashing.

The woman eyes me as I turn back. "Lin Mulan, I'm Han Daiyu. I'm a medic here.

Her eyes drag over me, assessing me from head to toe.

Her warrior uniform suggests she volunteered for her position.

"Yes, I'm here by intent. I work with one of the generals on his team. I've been assigned here while he's working with your new lieutenant as a liaison."

"Xiao Liling," a smaller girl introduces herself. Her brown hair is braided up, twisting around her head in a traditional style far too fancy for a warrior. "I wasn't supposed to be here."

"The general and his men will protect you, child," Daiyu says. "You'll be safe as a cook."

She'll be safe until Chen's army finds her and turns her into a concubine...if she's that fortunate and they don't do worse.

"And who might you be?" I ask the shy girl in green kimono. She tips her head up slightly and a long strand of white hair drops in front of her face. She reaches up to tuck it before answering.

"I am Feng Song. My mother is a seamstress—it's all I can offer the army in exchange for their protection. I'm thankful that dragon picked me up during the fight and took me to safety—I just didn't think safety meant rushing *into* the war."

"The general was quite pleased to hear you could mend the army's clothing, Song," Daiyu reminds her. "Everything will be alright. You'll be safe with us."

The woman glances up at me. "They're a bit nervous. They weren't meant to be here, but they'll do just fine once we get started. What precisely do you do?"

She appears to be softening. Behind me, everything goes silent save for the general.

"We come from a merchant family," I reply. "I can help you as a medic, and I can also offer the best tea in all of the Yan Liu province."

"Is that so?" She chuckles. "We'll speak more after the general is done."

We turn to face our leaders as they address their makeshift army.

"Under different circumstances, you would have received more training to learn how to work with each other in dragon form. These, however, are not normal circumstances."

Keung shifts next to the general, swaying his hair. The single braid I added this morning still resides in his locks—he had watched me so closely as I wove his hair through my fingers to create it—a reminder of me. I certainly didn't mind the way he gazed at me as I worked.

"I was not meant to lead your army, but my men and I will now be staying with you," The general addressees us. "The honor was to be passed to my son, Lieutenant General Yu Keung, and will be once we separate from you again. You are still to report to him with the utmost respect. He will oversee the day-to-day aspects of the army while my men and I strategize the overall war and report back to the imperial generals."

His words fade out as I register his last statement: Keung is his son.

Keung had never spoken of his father to me, much less that he was the leader of the imperial army. Nor did Keung tell me he would become the general of *this* army—I knew he was in leadership, but not to this extent.

His father—*the general*—continues speaking, back straight as an arrow. I'm overwhelmed by the notion of meeting and being dismissed by Keung's father so quickly, though I'm sure he doesn't know about us.

"We will travel in the mornings and train in the afternoons," General Yu continues. "Fighting while tired will push us, but traveling after training would be foolish."

"Lieutenant General Yu will now address you. The generals and I have business to attend to." The general pauses. "Prepare yourselves, men. We will push you hard because Chen's army will push you harder. If you die as we cross these mountains, no one will stop Chen from murdering us all as he escapes with the black jade blossom."

He steps off the makeshift platform someone set up for him and walks toward a large tent that has miraculously appeared off to the side—our men work quickly.

"We will use afternoons to familiarize ourselves with our fellow dragons and learn how to fight as a singular unit. You're all trained—now you just need to learn to work together," Keung takes over, stepping forward. His voice is more commanding than usual; deeper as well.

"We will have teams of men on lookout at all times. Everyone else will train—first on bo staffs, then with scales."

A cheer rises up from the crowd as he speaks of our scales. It's pride and comradery wrapped into one. Jinhai shouts beside me.

"Before you are split up and given assignments, I will make one thing very clear. There are women in our presence. They are to be cared for and protected. We may gain more of them along the way. Should I hear even a whisper I don't like, you'll pay the price." He pauses. "*And* should I *not* hear of it, you would do well to remember that these women are the ones who will be taking care of you when Chen's army scorches you."

"Well *that* doesn't put a target on our backs," Liling mutters. She's not as quiet as I thought she would be for someone who '*isn't supposed to be here.*'

"We'll protect each other," Daiyu says just loud enough for our group to hear. "I know how to fight and something tells me Mulan has some training behind her as well."

"Good call. Mulan can be *merciless* when she wants to be." Jinhai turns to her, making a joke. He leans forward, smiling. "Hi, I'm Lin Jinhai."

"Forgive my twin." I roll my eyes. "He doesn't know his place."

"She punched me one too many times growing up. I now live in fear." He grins flirtatiously. Liling giggles.

"You're going to be a troublemaker, aren't you?" Daiyu asks. She sounds amused, but her eyes suggest otherwise.

"I'll stay out of your way, Miss Han," Jinhai promises. "I can't say that I won't be seeing a lot of Miss Xiao and Miss Feng, though. I'm certain to need a seamstress when my muscles bust out of my uniform."

Song blushes deep red as Jinhai turns his attention on her. I move to grab my brother's arm to reel him in but miss as he sways, knowing my thoughts too well.

"Oh, I doubt it's your muscles that will bring you to Miss Feng at first...*Jinhai, was it?*" Liling jumps into the conversation, narrowing her eyes and smirking at my brother. "I think it will be your gut busting out of your uniform."

Jinhai pulls back like she slapped him making her laugh.

"I'm the best cook you'll ever meet." She looks him

over arrogantly, clarifying her point. "But I'm sure your muscles will be an issue, too."

She's definitely not the quiet young lady I thought she was a moment ago.

"Soldier?" Keung's deep voice booms behind us, prompting Jinhai to bow and scamper off to his team. He takes his place alongside Ning and Wei. "Ladies, are you aware of your assignments?"

"Yes, Lieutenant." Daiyu takes charge once again. "If it pleases, Lieutenant, I'd also like to train the women so they are prepared should they need to protect themselves if the battle comes to us."

"You've been trained?" Keung looks surprised as he appraises her.

"Yes, sir. Some of our fathers thought it wise to train their daughters to defend the village should the need arise, as it did today. The general is aware of this particular talent of mine, though it has not been used yet."

"Very well." Keung nods.

"I'd like to train with the men, Lieutenant," I say boldly. It's strange calling him anything other than his first name. It sounds so foreign on my lips. It must seem forced to him as well because the corner of one side of his lips moves—thankfully the side away from where the women can see. "My father trained me well and if I'm going to be in a combat situation, I'd like to make sure I'm ready."

"I don't need her to help with Miss Xiao and Miss Feng," Daiyu agrees. "If she wants to get beat up by the men, that's fine with me."

"I hardly think I'm going to get beat up." I turn to her, my competitive side coming out. She raises an eyebrow in challenge to see what I'll do in front of our commanding officer.

"Very well. You may train with your brother," Keung interjects. "Speaking of your *brother*, I need to have a word with him. Come."

He steps away and I hurry to follow behind him, catching up within a few steps. Dark blue is a good color on him. He clasps his hands behind his back, refusing to look at me.

"I worry about you being here," he murmurs. "And since when have you known how to fight?"

"Always," I respond. "My father wanted me protected."

"I see I have much to learn."

"You kept the braid," I switch the conversation, trying to hide my smile.

He turns slightly to me, softening. "Of course I did. It means a great deal to me."

Keung turns back quickly, taking on his commanding presence again. "Lin Jinhai! A word."

Jinhai looks over quickly and jogs to us, leaving his

team to work without him. He looks at me curiously.

"Your sister says your father trained you both?"

"Yes, sir," Jinhai replies, hands behind his back like a good soldier.

"She will further train with you then."

"Yes, sir."

Keung nods, appreciating his new position overseeing the army and the power that comes with it. "I need to have a word with you about your twin."

"Sir?" Jinhai holds perfectly still. We can't let him get caught in a lie, especially to our commanding officer.

"Where is he? He should be training too."

"He will only join us in dragon form, sir. It's too easy to be caught otherwise. I cannot question General Lin's orders." Using our father as an excuse...a wise choice.

"Then I will speak to him alone," Keung suggests.

"I'm sorry, sir—"

"I will speak to him *alone*, soldier.

Jinhai swallows. "Of course, sir."

The men around us call out directions, coaching each other on how they fight and what to do to improve their stances and strikes. Bo staff clanks against bo staff. Sword against sword.

"Where is he?"

"I don't know, sir." Jinhai is being cornered.

I tug on Keung's sleeve before realizing that's not

something I can do. I drop it. "Lan is known for wandering off to meditate and scout the area around us. I'm sure he'll be back by nightfall, Keung, um, Lieutenant."

I'm going to have to watch my words in public. Keung's body tightens next to me at my slip.

"I'd like to speak to him when he arrives. Bring him to me."

"Of course."

The lieutenant walks away to a nearby group and steps into the ring they've formed to fight against a man twice his size. We watch as he easily brings him to his knees.

"How do we handle this?" Jinhai whispers.

"We get you away from the other men and you play both roles."

"Easy enough," he muses, rolling his eyes. He motions to the men ahead of us. "You know you're going to have to fight these guys, right?"

"So?" Irritation creeps into my neck, warming it. "I'm perfectly capable of taking care of myself."

"Oh, I know." Jinhai turns to smirk at me. "I just meant to take it easy on them—we don't need them out of commission for the real fight."

He winks before snatching up a bo staff and tossing it

to me. He grabs another for himself and rushes into the ring. "Who's next, gentlemen?"

I'm tempted to step into the ring with him, but that would only lead to people saying he was going easy on me—that's the last thing I need. Instead, I follow Keung to the circle next to my brother where he's easily winning against a second man.

Wei steps into the circle just as I step up to join the men. My brother's friend eyes me as Keung waves me into the makeshift ring to spar. Wei twirls his staff and raises an eyebrow at me.

"Go easy on me, kid," he whispers, stepping around me for show.

"Yeah, sure." One corner of my mouth tugs up in a restrained grin. Most of us from our village have trained together—we know how we work. I may be the only female dragon aside from my mother, but thankfully, I'm not the only girl who was trained to fight. Though, that means, the only person I might impress today would be Keung—who has no idea what I'm capable of doing—and perhaps some of the men from the other villages that joined us or came with the generals' teams.

Wei and I position ourselves and bow. Holding my staff in both hands, I stare him down, waiting for him to strike first. Wei brings his staff down and I lift mine horizontally to block him. He towers over me, even taller than my brother or Keung—with his short, burnt orange hair, he looks strikingly different than both as well.

He swings his staff to strike low, but I block him and rock back for power before the next strike. The staffs collide with a sharp smack, meeting in the middle as we face in opposite directions.

"Warming up, Mulan?" Wei rears back, preparing to thrust the bo staff at me.

I shift my stance back, moving my feet to prepare for the block. Moving my right leg forward, I keep my hand low on that side. My opponent slides his hand on the bo staff and spins it, stepping toward me. I retreat, spinning mine as well. After a few steps, we move our left sides forward and collide again.

"Ready to take this up a bit?" I ask. He nods.

Wei acts as the aggressor, forcing my staff to the ground. He forces the bo staff up, trying to hit me, but I duck. The tall boy crosses behind and attempts to hit low, but I jump, causing him to miss.

Wei reminds me of Jinhai but with shorter hair. I'm not close with any of my brother's friends, but if pressed, I approve of Wei more than the rest of them.

"Come on, Mulan, stop holding back," he says quietly enough that no one else hears. He attempts to hit me in the face, but I block him, holding the staff vertically as I step into the hit.

As Wei steps away, I twist, kicking in the air unexpectedly and move forward, striking with my staff as he steps back. I hear a muffled sound from Keung as he watches.

I bring my staff down, attempting to strike from overhead, but Wei moves and blocks me as the ring of men shifts, cheering and calling to us.

Moving back, Wei attempts to hit my feet. I use my staff to stop him, rotating it back out of the way. He comes back, attempting to hit my mid-section. I block on the right, then the left as the men around us cheer.

"She's good," Keung says to someone. I disregard him, keeping my focus.

As Wei comes at me again, I strike from underneath, knocking his staff into the air above his head. He catches it, spinning the bo staff. "Feeling good about yourself?"

"Not yet," I reply.

We both spin our staffs and attack again. I strike and kick, twirling my staff and body over and over until I finally knock Wei to his knees. He kicks, nearly knocking me down as well. I ignore the background noise and focus on finishing the fight.

I miss his last move and he pulls my feet out from under me. Walking over, he helps me up. "That was close, Mulan. You're improving every time I see you."

We bow and step aside for the next pair to take their places.

"We'll have to get you something else to wear, Lin Mulan," Keung says quietly as I walk by. He drops his voice quieter so no one can hear him add, "You look beautiful, but that kimono is going to hold you back."

I had nearly forgotten I wasn't wearing the same uniform the rest of the men had reported to the Center in. Only Liling, Song, and I aren't dressed properly for war. I nod and Keung nods back, allowing me to pass.

For the rest of the afternoon, I train until I feel like my legs will give out, and worry about how we're going to trick Keung into believing my fake brother exists.

Deep navy blue fills the sky as gray wispy clouds float across the full moon. The stars sparkle as I push Jinhai toward the trees.

"Are you sure I should have my hair up? If we're supposedly switching places, shouldn't we be identical?" he whispers.

"It's fine, Jinhai. You're only supposed to look alike when you're switching places, but don't you think someone who lives in the shadows would want to differentiate himself at least *a little* when he's not playing a role?

"I guess."

"You started this, Jinhai. Just speak a little differently and we should be okay," I assure him.

"I started this to protect you and the family, Mulan." His lips twitch in annoyance. Jinhai has always been good about solving immediate problems, but sometimes he forgets the long-term fallout and ends up getting himself into even more trouble."

We part ways.

The trees sway in the breeze. With the mountains in the distance, it looks like a scene from a painting. A few flower petals fall from the blossoms on the trees, landing gracefully on the grass as I walk.

Lanterns blink near the tents, marking the paths as people walk from fire to fire and tent to tent talking. It's nearly time to sleep—we have another early morning—which means the meeting with Jinhai as Lan will be short.

The meeting tent is lit up brightly. Silhouettes of men dance against the fabric as they pour over maps and discuss where to direct the army to safely pass the mountains where the enemies and rebels lie in wait to prevent us from taking the black jade blossom back and restoring our life source to the land.

Sensing my approach—or maybe just to get some air—Keung steps outside. Another man steps out with him—his father.

I drop my smile and bow. Keung turns to his father and nods. The general returns his gesture and turns on his heels to walk away as Keung steps up to me.

"He is here, Lieutenant."

As I straighten, Keung grins at my formality. "Good."

He motions for me to take the lead. We keep distance between us as we walk among the shadows cast by the moon, lanterns, and fire. His hair sways in front of him in the breeze, as does mine.

"I see you found more suitable clothing," he comments, glancing over. "*Pity*."

Blush creeps into my cheeks and I'm grateful the firelight hides it in the shadows and orange glow. Daiyu lent me one of her uniforms until we pick up more supplies in the next village and Song can alter one for me.

"Where is your brother, exactly?" He leans forward, looking around as we approach the line of trees.

"Further in." I wave my hand. "We don't need anyone seeing him—he's so private."

We duck into the moonlit trees and make our way through them, careful not to trip on roots.

"So...then...there's no one here for the next few minutes..." he says slowly.

"No, I suppose n—"

"Good." He cuts off my words as he lunges at me.

Chapter 5

I LAND HARD AGAINST A TREE, KEUNG'S LIPS AGAINST mine. His hand grasps at my hip, the other at the back of my neck, cradling my head.

"Is this okay?" he whispers as he greedily kisses me.

I nod, giggling as his lips prevent me from speaking. Wrapping one hand around his neck like he has mine, I leave the other to rest on his chest. He only lingers for a minute, but that's all we need for his eager lips to leave us both gasping for air and dazed.

"I hate that you're in this war, Mulan, and it's killing me to stay away from you, but I'm so glad you're here." He breathes his words wistfully.

"My heart shattered when you left this morning, Keung," I whisper.

"We'll figure this out. For now, we should go meet

your brother." He pulls away slowly, clearly not wanting to release me.

My hair moves, following the path of his hand where he tugs his fingers through it. I wait until he's far away and the strands fall back to my chest before I step away from the tree—thank goodness Jinhai isn't here to witness this.

My heart slams into my chest as Keung sighs, dropping the hand he's holding out to me, waiting to walk me through the woods. This is going to be difficult.

"He's this way...I think." I point, allowing him to lead. I'm not sure where Jinhai is hiding, just that it would be several minute's walk in to avoid being overheard by other soldiers.

We walk far enough that I'm confident my brother didn't see anything he shouldn't. Jinhai steps out from behind a tree, appearing like a hero in a storybook with pages decorated in ancient-looking paintings. He tips his head sideways, appraising Keung.

"Sister," he greets me formally. He bows to the lieutenant.

Well, Lan is...interesting.

"Lin Lan," Keung addresses him. "Your brother tells me you wish to keep your existence a secret."

"It is the best tactic for surprising the enemy, yes." Lan is apparently a very stern version of Jinhai.

"Very well, how do you propose we train you?"

"Jinhai and I have been switching places for years without anyone knowing and we grew up with half those men. People assume we're both him...it allows us to be in two places at once."

"Or for one of them to get out of doing work," I interject.

"The jade dragon will show up because they've already seen him, and one of us will be there in this form," my brother says, ignoring me.

"He'll travel with us though?" Keung tries to get his facts straight.

"No, I'll follow after," Jinhai informs him. "I won't be walking with you, and we need to ensure the enemy doesn't see me transform should they find us when we shift. Now, Lieutenant, if that is all..."

Keung grimaces, obviously uncomfortable with the arrangement. I would be too if I were him, but the title of general commands too much respect to be ignored, even if Father is retired—the people of Yan Liu may not know of his heroics in the last war, but the leadership knows to cater to his wishes. The province owes him that.

"Out of respect for the great General Lin, I will go along with the plan, but remember, you answer to us."

"Of course, sir." Jinhai bows. "Please see that my sister returns to her tent safely. Allow me to walk you to the edge."

Jinhai gives me a knowing look. Or, maybe I misread his gaze and he really means to inform me that he wants to be closer to the tents so he doesn't have to wait as long to reappear as himself.

We walk in silence through the woods. Fireflies blink around us. The walk out is much faster than the walk in with my brother looming behind us.

Jinhai stops at the edge, waiting behind a tree for us to get far enough away that he can sneak out. Keung doesn't slow, to his credit, bidding me good night once we reach the edge of the camp.

The fires crackle as I make my way back to the women's tent to get to know my new roommates.

"The spies have returned with word of enemy encampments. The passages between the mountains are traps. We cannot fly over them because they'll be waiting for us!" The general shouts commands as the sun comes up.

The dew soaks into my shoes, chilling my feet. The lanterns have been pulled from the tents and several men are collapsing what is left of the temporary lodging.

The men with supplies joined us in the middle of the night from the nearby village. They look exhausted as they fight to listen to the general's words. They'll be transported on dragon back once we start to move to allow them to rest after rushing through the night to reach us before we moved out.

With orders given, we spread out and help load the dragons. The men take turns carrying the supplies on their backs. Some of the men remain in their human form to help tie on the supplies to the backs of the dragon's responsible for them. Daiyu and I assist before climbing on.

Jinhai shakes in his dragon form before allowing me up, stretching his muscles out. I pat his neck as I hold onto his spines to ensure I don't fall off as he takes flight.

"Wait, let me come with you. Spare one of the other men so he can help later." Daiyu walks up to us, turning just before reaching me and move's to Jinhai's head. "May I?"

The blue dragon jerks his head, motioning to his back. Once she's settled behind me, Jinhai takes off more gracefully than I ever could and lifts into the sky.

The villages are small below us. People run into their homes the moment they see the army above their heads. We fly quietly without any fanfare or announcements so as not to upset them or give away our position should Chen's men miraculously not see us in the air.

Daiyu interrogates me on medical knowledge. When she's finally satisfied, she moves on.

"Tell me about your village," she asks. "I had only just arrived when the Zhao Wu warriors attacked your Center. It looked different than mine."

"How so?" I question, wondering what part she means. I've traveled much of Yan Liu with father and it's all relatively the same, given some of the featured colors.

"More gold."

"We're closer to the capital. I've traveled a little for work and I've noticed the closer you get to the capital, the more ornate everything becomes. It's also why we weren't called to the war until now—we're further away from the fighting."

I wait to see if she reacts to the emperor sparing the richer villages near his palace. She doesn't.

"Where did you come from, Daiyu?"

"I'm from the outer province. My family sent me to live with my grandparents, but after seeing so many men come back wounded, I volunteered my services. One of the generals took a liking to me and allows me to stay nearby. I've traveled a lot during the war, but after the last battle, they decided to send the general to work here with the lieutenant and he brought me with him."

"Are you lovers?" The bluntness of my question surprises me and I jerk back toward Daiyu. "I'm sorry, that's personal."

"That's *very* personal. But no, we're not lovers. He

just knows I'm good at my job and we have an understanding. I think he feels safer about his postings when I'm nearby to help should the need arise."

Jinhai dips in the sky, prompting us to grab onto the spikes on his neck and side. He makes a noise in apology.

"Do you ever look down and just wonder what the people are like down there?" Daiyu suddenly murmurs. I turn to find her leaning over to look at the ground below us as we pass over a village. "They're so small, just going about their lives. The pagodas, the gardens, the fountains. Merchants selling their wares. Children playing in the meadows without a care...but the adults linger nearby with weapons in hand, waiting and watching should the enemy surprise them."

Darkness creeps into her voice as she speaks as if she's seen it happen. "Did that happen to your village?"

She pauses for a long time before answering. "Yes. Chen's men snuck in one night and waited until the day had begun to creep out and start murdering the village. It started in the marketplace and the slaughter spread quickly until we realized what was happening and our dragons took them out. I was sent away the next day. The war had only started a month before, but it was the catalyst for a lot of what came next for our people."

"I'm so sorry, Daiyu." The tragedy tugs at my heart, but it's not uncommon.

Jinhai dips again, lowering with the weyr as they prepare to land beyond the village. The children below us look up and run toward their homes as they notice the approach. Several older men wave to us, passing on blessings for our battle ahead.

"I saw you fighting yesterday. You've been trained well."

"I've been studying the warrior's way a long time. My parents wanted us prepared." I brush my hair back over my shoulder. My arm brushes over my knee with the movement. Pants may be more functional, but I miss my kimono.

The dragons pull their wings back, slowing their flight. Angling toward the open field, they take turns landing. As soon as we're on the ground, we scramble off my brother's back and rush to unload the dragons carrying supplies so they can shift and rest.

"I hear men are joining us here," Daiyu comments as she pulls a pack down and sets it in the grass.

"That's good," Jinhai replies, stepping to my side to help me remove a heavy tent from a purple dragon's back —I still don't know what all of the men look like in their transformed states, but I have to learn soon so I know who not to fight in battle.

We place the tent pieces on the ground. The men will

gather the supplies and put them on carts from the village to make our way up the mountain.

Wind pushes through the meadow, dropping blossom petals on our heads. It whispers, calling us closer to our destiny. I shiver against it, even though I'm not cold.

"Hello," Liling greets us. We look up as she joins us.

"Liling, did you leave Song on her own again?" Daiyu looks horrified. She rushes off to find the fragile girl, mumbling about Liling's manners.

"She should probably watch that since I'm the one cooking for her from now on," Liling jokes. She leans in toward my brother. "Perhaps I'll have to make something special for you and your sister later."

My body stiffens as my eyes narrow and whip over to her. I misjudged her when I first met her, but I can see her clearly now and I don't like her flirting with my brother.

"They've arrived!" a man's yell interrupts. "Load up!"

Jinhai grins at Liling quickly and then snatches up the tent pieces and moves them toward an open cart to help load it. *I'm going to have to put a stop to this rather quickly.*

We work hastily to load the wagons. Some of the carts are ornamental, taken from the wealthy families of the village, while others are more functional. Some are attached to horses, though most are dragged by the men. It will be a miracle if we can train this afternoon after this type of work. I take my place by my brother and the cart he's carrying and fall in line.

"Hello, beautiful." A man sidles up next to me. "What's a girl like you doing in a war? Here to entertain us?"

"I wouldn't speak to her like that if you don't want an ear cut off," Jinhai comments, glancing at the man around me from the corner of his eye. "She's a warrior, just like you and me, and a vicious one at that."

"Are you now, pretty?" He steps closer, eyeing me. He smells stale and outdated. The hair on the back of my neck prickles. I refuse to speak to him. *If only I could shift now.* "Well, just because you're good in battle doesn't mean you can't be good other pla—"

"I'd like a word with you, soldier." Keung's voice cuts him off as I turn to handle the situation.

The man turns, surprised, and stumbles over his words. "Yes, Lieutenant."

"*Better him than me,*" Jinhai mumbles as the man falls from our view. "And *definitely* better him than *you.*"

"And just what did you anticipate I'd do?" I challenge.

"We need our warriors, Mulan. You can't take them out of play. At least the lieutenant will keep that in mind. He's more level-head than you."

"As if *you* would know."

"The lieutenant knows we need every man alive and

able to fight if we're going to get the black jade blossom back from Chen and force the rebels out of Yan Liu—and preferably out of Zhao Wu and restore the rightful leadership again. The lieutenant won't touch him if he's smart."

"We've been trying for the last year to restore the emperor of Zhao Wu-before the black jade blossom was taken and our priorities changed, that is. Do you really think we can force Chen out of both *our* kingdom *and* theirs?" Liling asks, walking up to us.

"Aren't you supposed to be riding?" I ask, annoyed. I had ensured she was sitting in a cart far away from us before we started out.

"I got tired of sitting and thought I'd walk for a little while. You two seemed like you'd be good company." She practically skips between us. "I saw the Lieutenant drag that awful man away. Did you know he sniffed your hair before approaching you?"

My eyes widen. The skin on the sides of my eyes feels like I got too close to a sparkler and little dots of fire have dropped onto it, while my cheeks warm. I start to sputter a response but Jinhai cuts me off.

"I'll kill him *after* the war."

"How brave and protective of you." Liling giggles. I might have to kill *her* after the war too. Perhaps my twin and I can share a cell for our offenses.

The mountain looms ahead, rising spectacularly out

of the ground. Clouds swirl around the top of it, blocking the tip from view. The front of the line begins to climb the path leading up the face of the mountain as the breeze picks up.

A gust of wind hits, pushing my hair back harshly. Then another. Then another so strong it nearly knocks us over.

"Get down!" Jinhai suddenly screams. "It's a dragon!"

Chapter 6

THE DRAGON'S SCREAM FILLS THE AIR, RATTLING everything from the mountainside to the village. Its fiery breath scorches the ground, lighting up some of the carts and men.

Smoke instantly fills the sky, giving away our position to the enemy that our spies have told us are waiting on either side to shoot us down—we can't sneak over the mountain now.

The burning soldiers scream, their agony overtaking the sounds of the dragon's wings as it arches and prepares to throw fire again. Soldiers run, trying to avoid its path.

Men from the front transform, racing toward the silver dragon only to be shot down by Chen's men from deep within the valley near the mountain's slope. They fall, nearly crushing more of our men.

"The cannons!" Keung shouts from several yards

away. The rude man is no longer with him—I catch sight of him scampering away, blood dripping from his mouth.

"Mulan, hurry!" Jinhai yells, tugging at me.

I rush behind him, leaving the cart in our wake. Liling has disappeared into the crowd somewhere. Jinhai grabs a cannon from another cart and we work together to set it up and light it. We aim it at the dragon in the sky, still terrorizing our men.

Next to us, a fourth and fifth cannon are tossed to the ground and angled at the beast. They sizzle for a moment before exploding, taking off toward the silver dragon. The first two shots miss as the dragon darts into the sky to blend into the wispy clouds.

Right before our cannon fires, Jinhai and I jerk it upward at the same time, angling for where we think it is in the sky. An explosive shriek erupts overhead, and dragon scales splatter down at us. The dragon cries, reemerging from the clouds as it fights not to fall.

The third cannon misses, but the fourth has enough time to reposition itself before the explosion. The dragon launches a stream of fire at our men, hitting two of them and another cart. The fourth cannon's mark is true, striking the side of the beast, delivering the final blow needed to end it.

As it falls, I can see where Jinhai and I struck its wing and shoulder making it hard for the dragon to fly. Ning's cannon has hit it more directly on the opposite side leading to its downfall.

It collapses on the ground as our men run to it. He transforms, shifting into his human state, long hair covering his face.

"It's a woman!" one of the soldiers calls, pulling back at his discovery.

Rumbles go up through the group. With the silver dragon grounded, Chen's army stops firing, pulling back.

"She's alive!"

Everyone's eyes widen.

"Mulan, go!" Jinhai grabs my arm and pushes me forward. I stumble, forgetting I'm serving as a medic to the army.

Throwing myself on the ground, I search her body for weapons. I throw them aside as I locate them for someone else to pick up. Once I'm sure she's clear, I assess her wounds. For being so badly damaged in the air, her human form has done remarkably well...perhaps an advantage to having the black jade blossom on her side.

"Let me go!" she howls as her eyes blink open. The woman claws at me, scratching my arm.

She hisses in my face, moving so quickly that she nearly collides with me as she sits up. I scramble backward, kicking her side as hard as I can in the process. The dragon woman screams, cursing at me.

"I'm trying to help you!" I scream at her.

"I don't want your help—" her words are cut off as a bo staff slams into the back of her skull. She sinks forward.

"Bind her," Keung commands, walking up behind her into my line of sight. Ning and another man rush forward to hold her in place as one of the other men stretches the cord around her. Shackles are placed over her wrists to prevent her from shifting—even if she could shift in that state, she would be so hobbled in dragon form that it would mean instant death or capture.

"We need to hurry!" Keung continues. "The general is holding the path for us, we must move forward!"

So, Keung's father has the power to hold a shield barrier in place. I didn't realize the general had such a powerful gift—few dragons do. If he can blind Chen's men from us for a few moments, we can start on the path to the mountain without being caught. With any luck, they won't be able to track us until it's too late.

Every man grabs a cart and rushes forward. Some pull, some push from behind to move them over the rocky terrain. Jinhai lurches forward and I lean into the back of the cart, helping him force it along.

"That was smart to clear her of weapons," Keung says, rushing alongside me to help. He lowers his head to put more muscle into it. I glance at his taught arm next to me.

"What will happen to her?" I ask him, knowing she won't give anything up easily.

"We'll torture her for information if necessary. She doesn't seem like the type to give much up."

"Ask Daiyu if she has herbs to help. I've been told there are flowers and herbs that can make people feel calm enough to speak their minds freely." I rattle off a few types and where they're predominantly found. "Perhaps she has some."

"Have you tried this before?"

We both grunt at the same time as we force the cart over a large rock. I release my grip for a moment to get a better hold.

"Faster!" Keung lifts his head and shouts to the group. "It won't hold much longer!"

"Will your father be alright?" I ask quietly. My words are nearly drowned out by the carts crashing around us.

"This will drain him. He won't be able to do anything else for us for a while. We'll need to protect him."

"Sure seems like an interesting way to introduce a girl to your family," I joke, trying to keep him from being worried.

"We'll get to that," he replies seriously. Then he winks.

"If your father has this power, what did you inherit?"

"Nothing of value, I'm afraid. Keep pushing, Mulan, we're almost there."

The slope takes a sharp turn and we rush up the face of the mountain to the hidden paths within the trees and rocks where Chen's men can't find us unless they're in dragon form. They won't risk being shot down, so we're safe until we leave the mountainside.

The leaves rattle loudly on the trees behind us.

"The protective barrier has fallen. We're on our own now," Keung whispers. "I have to speak with the general."

I nod, releasing him from helping me as the pace slows now that we've reached the mountain.

"See what you can get out of the silver dragon when she wakes back up...*you're good at getting people to tell you everything.*" Keung summons over a soldier to take my place and motions me toward the barred cart carrying the silver dragon woman several over.

Another lieutenant joins me, representing the command. He walks several paces behind to observe and intervene if needed. His presence is mostly comforting.

After a few minutes, the woman starts to stir again. She attempts to raise a hand to move her curly black hair out of her face and curses when she finds herself chained to the cart.

"I'll burn you all," she growls, not having noticed me yet.

"Will you?" She startles at my words. "Why are you here?"

"As if I would tell you." The silver dragon woman glances around, taking in the airy trees. "The mountains."

"Yes, despite your best efforts, we made it."

She stares at the trees, watching them bend on the breeze. Crickets chirp around us and birds call to one another longingly. A fine mist swirls around our feet.

"They say this mountain is cursed…"

"They don't," I correct her. "They say your emperor is losing the battle as we speak."

"My king is not."

"No?" I ask casually. "We haven't seen him in months. I heard he had died or has been hiding in his palace."

I'm fully aware Chen has been hiding behind his army with the black jade blossoms as he attempts to kill our nation and prevent us from taking back our life source.

"*Your* emperor hides, girl. Ours is on the battlefield slaying your dragons."

"No battlefield that I've seen," I scoff, hoping to get a location from her.

"None that you *will* see." She catches on to my plan. "You'll be dead long before he finds your men. *Why are you here, girl?* You can't fly, so what good can you be?

Unless you're a concubine. Perhaps to the general himself. Though, I hear he doesn't have the—"

"Enough, women," the lieutenant steps up. "Why were you sent here?"

"To burn men like you." She looks him up and down until the cart bumps over a rock, jostling her enough for her hands to dart out to find something to hold her in place lest she crash into the bars.

"Why *you* and not one of their *more-skilled* warriors?" the lieutenant asks.

"What makes you think I'm not a skilled warrior?" She crawls forward as far as her chains allow. The woman pulls her lips back in an attempt to be seductive, but the teeth filed to points prevent that. The lieutenant sneers.

"You were so easily caught."

"Perhaps that was the plan." She grins evilly.

"It wasn't," I quickly jump in. "If that was your plan, this would have played out very differently."

"A war maker, are you?" She whips around to look back at me. "You hardly look old enough to be studying war tactics, much less planning them. You won't be getting anything out of me, girl. Though, perhaps I'll trade for some belladonna."

"If you were going to kill yourself, you should have aimed better when you fell out of the sky." She reels back at my words.

"A healer, then?" she guesses. Perhaps I should have allowed her to think I was a concubine and worked to gain her trust. "Such pretty hair. *All the boys* must be after you, little pet."

Her change is abrupt, setting me on edge. Maybe I can use it to my advantage.

"What must the little boys do to get your attention, healer?" Her words are long and drawn out, taunting me, baiting me to engage.

"I once had a boy bring me a lantern; red with a tassel of yellow," she murmurs watching me intently. "He lifted it into the air saying it was like our love and we watched it float into the sky. It mixed with hundreds of others, floating far away. He promised to take care of me, but I wasn't ready for that kind of commitment.

"We are the same, no?" she continues. "We do not need men. We are too...*powerful.*"

Ice courses through the veins in my wrists. *Could she possibly know my secret?*

"How do you know I don't have *many* boyfriends?" I reach down, grasping a handful of tall grass and begin weaving it together in my hands as I walk.

"Too proper for that. A *single lover* or you send them away." She looks me over. "Shouldn't you be married by now, little pet?"

"Perhaps I should be. Maybe I'll look for *your*

husband after we're done with you...*provide him some comfort.*"

"Good luck with *that* from the grave." She smirks.

"What is your name?" I ask, working the blades of grass in my hands. "I've traveled to Zhao Wu before the emperor fell and the kingdom was closed off, perhaps I know your family."

"Trying to determine if I'm a rebel from the province or one of his elite, *hm?* I sent my secrets away with that lantern into the night sky, little girl. I'm too smart for that."

"So I see, silver dragon. But *our* dragons are powerful too. You underestimate us."

"I shall rest now to heal my injuries." She nods dismissively at me. "We will meet again, little pet. I'll paint your body with your own blood when we do. Scales and swirls, perhaps."

The lieutenant slams his sword's broad side into the bars, rattling the woman. "If we wanted you to threaten our women, we would have allowed you into the villages."

She argues back as he motions me away from the women. From my place at Jinhai's side, I watch her raise her voice before tipping over and passing out, a dart sticking out of the back of her arm.

"They'll brand her," Jinhai explains. "Mark her as an enemy dragon so no one is fooled."

"They'll drug her," I reply. "They'll get their answers."

"Your idea, I assume."

"Faster than torture...probably." I set my hand on my brother's shoulder. This time yesterday, I was preparing to say goodbye to my brother in the Center. Much has changed in a single day.

Murmurs filter through the ranks over the next few hours until we find ourselves on the backside of the mountain. Our command gives orders to rest—we'll be finishing the journey in the dark in hopes of escaping the mountain without being seen.

"Come, sit with me, sister." Jinhai waves me over to a fallen tree. "We should eat something and rest."

I'm not nearly as tired as my brother, but I also didn't fly for hours this morning. The sun glitters on the edge of the mountain, sparkling off of trees and leaves, high-lighting radiant hair colors as if they were on fire. Everyone around me is ablaze with golden light and mountain mist.

I rest my head on Jinhai's shoulder and he wraps an arm around me. "We'll get back to them."

He knows me so well.

"Besides, Lan has our backs." My twin winks at me conspiratorially.

Beside us, men talk of the silver dragon woman and

what the imperial army does to woman who shift. "There are no women dragons born in Yan Lui. Any female with wings has to be a rebel working with Chen."

"We should cut off their wings when we find them!"

"We should lock them up and never release them!"

"Why not use them as concubines? The bindings would only help!" The men laugh.

"There are many ways to break a dragon, boys. I'm sure the army has been creative."

They continue their conversation as I restrain Jinhai from speaking his mind.

"Ignore them, they're fools," Wei says, sitting down on the fallen tree opposite us. Ning takes a seat by his side. "Did you two survive alright?"

"We're fine," Jinhai answers, still glaring at the men as they turn their conversation even more colorful.

"Hello again," Liling says, announcing herself as she sits down next to Wei, bouncing the tree branch.

Jinhai turns back around to face her, glare gone. Then, realizing there's another woman present, he takes the opportunity to lecture the men about priority in the presence of ladies. Liling looks impressed as he turns back gallantly.

My hair shifts behind me as someone disturbs the air.

"Lin Mulan, I'd like a report on the silver dragon." Keung towers over me. As I glance up, I see every muscle through the fabric of his uniform and consider myself a very lucky girl.

I stand, straightening my own uniform and follow him to the edge of the camp where we can speak privately without any prying eyes.

He grins.

Chapter 7

"WHAT DID YOU LEARN?" KEUNG TURNS TO ME, setting our priorities. He reaches down to pick up a bo staff and hands it to me.

"What's this?" I ask, taking it from him.

"We talk while we spar, Mulan." He says my name gently. "I didn't know you were trained so well. I want to see for myself how you do. You impressed me yesterday."

Amused, I take my place and bow to him. We rise at the same time and lift our staffs. Circling, he waits for me to strike first. I oblige.

"Her husband is dead," I inform him. "She caught me trying to decipher if she was a Zhao Wu rebel or originated from Chen's army. So, no information there."

"I heard she tried to rattle you," he comments, attempting to pull my feet out from under me.

I jump, lifting my staff to strike his head. "You mean threatening to paint my body with my own blood?"

"She *what?*" The admission causes him to pause and I use the opening to slam the end of my bo staff into his chest, nearly knocking him down. He staggers back, looking at me.

"It's fine, Keung, she can't touch me in those shackles, but even if she *could*, I'm perfectly capable of taking care of myself."

"Brave as you are, Mulan, you can't win against a dragon."

If only you knew, Keung.

He moves quickly, rushing at me with his staff. I raise mine up, blocking his attack, but he moves fast, attempting to overwhelm me. Jumping, I spin, kicking out with my foot until I connect with him. He brings his staff down on my hip, forcing me to the ground.

"You're good," he comments. "Let's see what else you've got."

"She called me *little pet*," I inform him as he runs at me. "And she said women hold power. She mostly rambled until they knocked her out.

"Now," I grunt, "I have a question for *you.*"

"Oh? Will I like this question, Lin Mulan?" He drops his voice flirtatiously. I smile and bat my eyelashes while reaching behind him with my staff and hit one of his legs.

"Can't say I don't like *that*." He grins.

I ignore his playfulness and ask my question.

"That man who was harassing me earlier...what did you do to him?" I bring the bo staff up, trying to attack while his hands are up. The staffs clink together loudly.

"We had a talk," Keung replies.

Pieces of debris and dust in the air sparkle as they float around my commanding officer, glittering in the early evening light. He's radiant as he moves, each graceful step reminding me I can't pause to watch him. I wonder what I look like in this light from where he stands sizing me up.

"One that left him bleeding?" I question, knowingly.

"I don't tolerate insubordination in my men, Mulan. I know his type. He wouldn't hesitate to drag one of you ladies off into the woods when no one was looking." He quickly adds, "Not you, of course—*you'd* kill him. But one of those small girls would be easy prey for him."

"So, you turned him into a lesson," I state. It's not a question.

"I did." He twirls his staff and strikes. I lunge, avoiding it and nearly knock it out of his hand with my next blow.

We both sweat from the exertion of the workout. Somehow it makes him even more attractive, while I fear it's doing the opposite for me.

Keung smirks as if he knows what I'm thinking and licks his lip quickly. He moves to the right and tries to strike. The setting sun blinds me and I nearly miss the block.

"Did you have to cut his tongue out to make a point, Keung?" I ask boldly. He looks shocked.

"His tongue is still attached, unfortunately." He grimaces. "I told him if he made a sound while we cut, I'd take the whole thing, but for your peace of mind, I only took the tip to make a point."

"In honor of me, *how kind*," I bait.

"I knew you'd be upset if I did worse."

Our staffs collide again, smacking loudly. The sound reverberates off the trees nearby.

"You restrain yourself for me, is that it?" I ask, annoyed. He shouldn't have cut the man.

"In more ways than one."

My jaw drops open. He smirks and sweeps my feet out from under me, sending me crashing to the ground on my backside.

"Time to head back." He reaches down offering me a hand. I'm not sure touching him right now is a good idea for either of us. "We'll do this again another time, Lin Mulan."

"Lieutenant."

The walk back is silent, crackling with lightning

between us. Of all the things we could have done in those woods, this might have been the most intimate.

"You were gone longer than I expected." Jinhai holds a blanket out to me.

"I was training."

I drape the blanket over the ground and lie down next to my brother. He watches me warily.

"He said he was impressed with my skills yesterday and wanted to see what I could do for himself."

"He thought I took it *easy* on you?" Wei gasps, sitting down next to me on his blanket.

I cover myself with the remaining part of the blanket, less for warmth, more because I'm surrounded by hundreds of men.

"No, that's not—"

"He needs to stay away from my sister," Jinhai cuts me off with his mumble.

Wei gives his friend a pointed look across where I lay. The two have a silent conversation and I roll my eyes, tucking myself to face Wei so I don't have to look at my twin. If I said anything now, it would just lead to an even bigger discussion while we're supposed to be attempting to sleep for two hours before we finish climbing down the mountain in the moonlight.

I run through the signals that Keung had assigned to the army yesterday after physical training had ended. We've drilled them over and over during our travels to ensure we all know how to fight when we're in dragon form without being able to speak. Jinhai filled me in on what I missed when I was called to help Daiyu before the meeting had finished.

I say it over and over in my head until it lulls me to sleep. My survival depends on it.

The air is crisp as we walk the backside of the mountain. The wind rushes by like a tunnel of air but doesn't hinder our travel.

Fireflies twinkle beside us, growing in number the further we sneak toward the ground. The crickets chirp loudly, wishing us the good luck they carry in their songs.

I look up, tracing the stars with my eyes. I've always had an obsession with the heavens and their tiny lights. It makes me feel safe and connected when I watch the stars.

"Careful," Jinhai whispers, pointing out a rock that would be easy to trip over. I turn, pointing it out to the person behind me.

Without lantern light, it's hard to see obstacles in our way. Jinhai thankfully passed off the cart to another soldier, leaving us to walk without exerting ourselves. Any of the men who intend to shift at the bottom to escape are taking it easy now to save their strength.

"The spies have said there is a small group of men waiting to help at the bottom of the mountain. They'll dispose of the carts and take the horses from us. Be prepared to leave anything that isn't necessary." The commanding officers inform us continually along the path so we're ready once we arrive at the bottom of the mountain.

"When we get down there, don't leave my side," Jinhai whispers sharply, his overprotective side coming out. He's barely ten minutes older than me, but he's convinced I should be several years younger.

"I'm not seven and this isn't our mother's home," I whisper back. I avoid saying we've been to Zhao Wu in case it comes back to haunt us later, even though I mentioned it to the silver dragon earlier— hopefully they'll assume I was lying to get information.

"I'm aware you aren't a child, Mulan, but Mother will kill me if anything happens to you out here." He holds up a tree branch for me to duck under. "Besides, I recall a few times I had to save you on our travels."

"Chasing off boys hardly counts as saving me," I comment.

"While the most *heroic* of my deeds, that's not what I meant." The tree snaps behind him, hitting Ning in the face. He chastises Jinhai before shoving his shoulder good-naturedly.

"I recall saving you when you chased after a little blonde girl and nearly drowned yourself in the process," I recall loud enough for the boys to hear behind us. They scoff at him, cracking jokes quietly.

"Careful, I seem to recall a certain..." He trails off, realizing he shouldn't bring it up. "*Number of things* you wouldn't want discussed, dear sister."

"Oh?" Wei teases. "A boy perhaps?"

"Does charming little Mulan have a boyfriend we don't know about?" Ning adds, elbowing me. I regret letting them walk with us.

If only you knew.

"No, no, genius. They're talking about their past. It must be some childhood love, isn't that right, Mulan?" Wei comments.

"Gentlemen, allow me to remind you that I hold sway with every eligible woman in the village and likely any other women you two stumble across and try to match-make yourselves with," I say in a sweet, quiet voice. "I wouldn't push it if I were you, boys."

"Apologies, Miss Lin." Wei acquiesces first, quieting. Ning follows his lead as I let out a chuckle.

Even so, Keung was my first kiss. I knew many boys as a child and young lady, but Keung was the first I ever counted as anything more than flirtation. None of them needed to know that though, especially my brother.

"We're here," the man ahead of us whispers. "Get ready."

Everyone stops walking, preparing for the first group of men to run out into the open. In theory, there's a group of spies waiting to help us at the bottom. If our intelligence is correct, Chen's men are at the other side of the mountain, waiting for us to breach, unaware that we've already conquered the climb—we tried to make it look like we'd turned back. We *should* be safe.

The general's men—the ones that came to collect our army—lead the way. Three of them on horseback quietly ride out into the moonlight-covered grass. Nothing stops them.

They press forward, moving toward a natural rock barrier. After a moment, they disappear behind it.

We hold still, waiting and watching, as the insects intensify their song of the night. After ten minutes, we send another team. Ten minutes after that, a larger team goes.

Within an hour, I'm near the edge of the mountain,

waiting for my turn to run to safety. I follow Jinhai down the path, holding his shoulder for support when we reach the steep drop off people without carts are using to expedite the process.

Keung snags my hand at the bottom, steadying me without anyone noticing. He squeezes it quickly before releasing it. As he drops his hand, he allows it to brush along my hip heavily, fingers grasping on for a moment until I have to pull away.

"Be safe," he says, quickly pointing out where to run. We wait for the clouds to cross the moon, creating deep shadows for us to run under.

Jinhai wraps an arm around my hip and pulls me along with him, staying low to the ground. Ning, Wei, and several others run behind us. The rock barrier seems to rise up out of the ground like the mountain had when we approached it. When we reach the far side, we see the soft orange glow of torches.

A man beckons to us. When we reach him, he wastes no time instructing us. "You're safe from here to the edge of the field. We have men ready to draw fire for you if necessary and put down any enemies that have eluded us.

"Run to the trees—your warriors are waiting there." He turns, pointing. "Don't stop."

"Thank you," I murmur before Jinhai pulls me away.

As we draw near to the trees, something in the sky catches my attention. "What is that?"

Jinhai looks up. "Is that a dragon?"

"They found us?" Ning yelps, shocked.

"Get to the trees!" Wei directs and we all run faster.

Bursting through the tree line, I pant from the run. Jinhai is out of breath too, which is unusual for him—he might not be as skilled in the air as I am, but he can run circles around me in human form.

"There's a dragon," I gasp.

"*Our* men," a soldier informs me. "The general decided if we take off here and fly as high as possible, they likely won't be able to see us while the sky is still black. We can get an hour in and cover more ground. We've sent quite a few men already."

"Looks like that's our cue, boys," Jinhai says, turning to grin. His wings aren't as strong as mine, but he loves being in the air more than anything but possibly that blonde girl he chased a few years ago.

"Over there." The soldier jerks his thumb over his shoulder, indicating the boys have to wait to shift.

Jinhai sighs.

We pick our way around the underbrush, ducking beneath dark tree branches that barely miss our faces. The nerves in my body tingle, wanting to shift and fly on my own, but I know I can't. Convincing them to calm takes all of my thought.

"I know," Jinhai whispers as he prepares to shift in the clearing hidden in the middle of the trees. "Soon."

I climb up his scales and settle. The air is much colder at night and the wind whips my hair behind me as we fly to our destination. The boys quickly catch up to the other dragons high in the sky and we form a silent line across the night sky, much too high to be seen.

Tipping my head back, I watch the stars as we travel, trusting my twin to keep us safe. *If only I could fly right now.*

In the distance, an orange glow burns like a tiny dot on the landscape—*war*—and we're flying right to it.

Chapter 8

"Get up, Mulan," Song says softly in my ear. I bolt up from my blanket, looking to see where the enemy is.

"Overreact much, Mulan?" Liling asks, looking over.

"The Lieutenant called for you and Daiyu." Song looks helpless kneeling on the edge of my blanket.

"Where is Daiyu?" I sit up, pulling back the edge of the blanket to release my legs.

"She went straight there with her kit and told me to wake you."

I mumble thanks and brush past the two smaller girls. Liling brushes her hair, weaving it intricately. "I'll bring him some food personally in a few minutes. I'm sure he needs it after last night."

Not bothering to do more than run my fingers through my hair to work out the tangles, I let it fly behind me as I rush to the general's tent with my medic bag in hand.

One of the lieutenants stands outside to grant passage into the general's quarters. He eyes me and nods, allowing me through.

The other generals stand around waiting for Daiyu to do her job. General Yu sits up on his cot and answers the medic's questions. She asks a few about his gift of creating a protective barrier, but the general doesn't share much with her.

Keung waits on the side. Every so often, he leans forward as if anxious to get involved, but then holds back to stay within his rank. The general may be his father, but Keung conducts himself within his ranking in the army—a subordinate.

Finally, Keung notices me as I hover near the door. One corner of his lips tugs up as he playfully leers at me. With all other eyes on the general and Daiyu, no one notices the way Keung's eyes slowly travel down over my body to the floor where my boots rest grounded and waiting to move me, and back up, slowly tracing every curve until he reaches my neckline. He pauses, eyes dragging over my shoulders slowly until he finally makes eye contact.

His lips part slightly, and he tips his head down just enough for his hair to shift so he can look out from under it at me. No one has ever been able to get my attention so easily.

"You just need to rest," Daiyu concludes, breaking Keung's spell over me. "No more *help* until it's built back up in you."

"Very well," General Yu says, waving her off. "If you're all quite satisfied that I'm not going to die, you may leave."

"Guess I wasn't needed after all," I mumble, turning to go.

"Oh, but *I* need you," Keung whispers in my ear, sneaking up behind me. "Meet me outside. Back of the tent."

He maneuvers around me, chatting with the generals. The sun is bright as I step out of the dark room, nearly blinding me.

I wait until no one is watching and slowly make my way to the side of the tent.

"Mulan?" A woman's voice startles me.

"Yes? Daiyu." I had nearly forgotten she was here. "I see you didn't need me after all."

"No, but I thought it was better to have you there in case I needed you to fetch something for me—I don't trust these boys to do anything properly when it comes to this. They'd run all the way to you and forget what they needed."

I chuckle. I don't disagree.

"Are you coming back with me?" she asks, nodding toward where we slept.

"No," I apologize. "I have some business to attend to. Sorry."

"Want me to take that back for you?" She holds out her hand for my bag. I give it to her, thanking her.

When I'm sure she's gone, I slip behind the tent to wait. Minutes pass before I hear Keung's voice.

"I'm meeting with a spy. I'll check in later."

He's backlit in the mid-morning sunlight when he appears. My lieutenant walks over to me quickly.

"*She's* a spy?" a second voice asks, booming.

Keung quickly whips around before he has a chance to take my hands. "She's our point of contact. I said I would check in with you later, General—"

"*Your father*—" the man cuts him off.

"—*is aware* that I'm going to meet with our spy. Do you need anything else, sir?" He's facing away from me, but I can tell he's glaring at his superior—a bold move.

"Let him go!" General Yu shouts from inside the tent. The fabric snaps as the breeze picks up. I'll have to remember how easily one can be heard through these tents during future conversations.

The man grumbles, retreating. Keung makes a face with wide, intent eyes as a signal to me. I keep very quiet.

"Have you spoken with him yet today?" he asks loudly, leading us away. "Anything to report?"

"I haven't spoken with him since before the mountain," I reply.

We pick our way around the fires that popped up to warm the men after their exhausting midnight flight. We keep up the guise of discussing the clandestine meeting we're not really attending—*at least I hope not since Jinhai isn't prepared to become Lan*—and make our way to the woods where we stopped to rest.

The men posted at the tree line nod as Keung passes with me trailing behind him. Along the way, he picked up bo staffs for us to work with. The lieutenant pauses to address the men.

"We're meeting with one of the spies. Should anything happen, only *you* should come find us. No one else. And be discrete." He points to one of the men, assigning him the pretend duty of searching for us in the woods should anything occur while we're away.

"Yes, sir." The man bows respectfully as we continue on.

"You really haven't heard from Lan?" Keung asks, guiding us around rocks and trees. "Did he fly with us last night?"

"I'm sure he joined at some point. He's always nearby." I brush my hair back realizing the nervous feeling in my stomach is starting to spread.

"And you just trust the jade dragon to show up when you need him?"

"Yes, the jade dragon is always there when we need him." I take Keung's hand as he reaches back for me. I've missed this part of our conversations.

"Forgive me for being so bold but he seems different than most of our dragons."

"Maybe." I try to be vague. "Are we coming out here to work or *something else*, Keung?"

He pauses in a space where the trees have grown far enough apart to give us room to spar. Light filters down in patches, dancing on the forest floor through the leaves and branches above us. If I angle myself correctly, I can use one of the tree trunks to launch myself off of in attack when the time comes.

"Can't it be both?" He chuckles. Sighing, he adds, "Mulan, you know what will happen if they catch us. I'm your commanding officer; we have to be careful."

"You're saying you want us to stop?" I ask flirtatiously. "You want to stay apart?"

I step toward him slowly, holding eye contact. Keung tracks my moves.

"We're alone now..." I raise a hand and run it up the front of his chest, resting it on his shoulder. I inch closer, daring him to kiss me. Usually he doesn't make me work this hard to get lost in his lips.

His arm slowly reaches around my waist, making me smile. Tipping his head, he moves toward me.

I jerk to the side as he throws me to the ground next to the bo staffs he dropped when he spun to face me in the clearing. Keung bends, grabbing one to spar. A satisfied smirk blossoms on his face for fooling me.

"I care very much about you, Lin Mulan, which is why I'm going to make sure you're ready for this battle. I won't let anything—even those alluring lips of yours—distract me from making sure you survive this."

Standing, I brush myself off.

"You're no fun, Lieutenant." I pout before grabbing the bo staff and whipping it in his direction. He blocks me, attempting to flip it out of my hand.

Leaping to my feet, we battle until I feel the fatigue setting in. Operating on very little sleep has made this difficult. We take turns bouncing off the trees, fighting for the upper hand, but neither of us yield.

"You're incredibly impressive, Mulan." He circles me, striking to the side.

"You can stop worrying about me, Keung. I can take care of myself in battle."

"Mulan, promise me you won't run into this fight. Assure me you'll stay with the women and care for our injured. I can't be distracted worrying for your safety when the time comes, and neither can your brother."

"I know my duty, Keung." I attempt to pull his feet out, but he jumps. Sweat trickles down my body as I lunge again.

"I could watch you do this all day. The way you move is magnificent."

"And I you, Keung. I prefer to see you win, which is a shame given you're tiring, and I have the upper hand."

The exhaustion must be making me bold. Perhaps it's the isolation.

He takes it as a challenge and rushes at me. We both take turns nearly falling, but in the end, it's me who collapses first, dragging Keung down with me.

The lieutenant raises himself up where he's tangled around my legs and waist from the fall and drags himself forward to lean over the length of me panting heavily.

"I hope you never have to use this, Lin Mulan," he whispers, pulling himself closer. "I pray the fighting never reaches you, but should it come and should you be taken, know that I will terrorize everything to the ends of the earth to get you back."

My hand goes up, lighting brushing his chest. "Keung."

I lean up to kiss him but pull back quickly as we're interrupted. Ning looks wild-eyed at us. His eyes dart back and forth between us as we try to catch our breath. My heart pounds in my ears so loudly I have to play his words over in my head before I can understand him.

"Apologies, Lieutenant." Ning quickly bows. He turns to me, scowling. "Your brother is going to *kill* you, Mulan."

He moves to glance at Keung one more time, sending a withering look in his direction, but doesn't say another word to his commanding officer.

Keung scrambles away from me, rising.

"You will not tell him *a thing*, soldier," he warns harshly. He releases a breath and softens his voice. "It won't happen again."

Ning doesn't turn around but pauses at the lieutenant's words. He nods, still facing away, and leaves the way he came.

Keung tears his gaze away to look at me, still on the ground. I'm sure I'm bright red after being caught in such a potentially compromising situation.

"Mulan," Keung whispers and hurries to me. He extends a hand and waits to help me up. "I'm so sorry."

"You didn't know we would be caught." I brush myself off, knocking decaying leaves from my uniform. "I'll handle things with my brother."

"No, Mulan." I look up and find the most heartbreaking eyes I've ever seen in my life. He takes me in his arms. "I'm sorry because he's right—we can't do this. I told you I could keep this separate, but I can't."

I try to speak, to soothe his fears, but he won't let me. Both arms wrap around me, holding me tightly to him as he tries to say goodbye to me.

"The best way to protect you is to keep our distance. We need to be focused in this fight. And what if someone else had seen us out here? What if the enemy found out who you are to me?"

He's clearly been thinking about this. He grows more agitated as he speaks.

"Knowing I lead this army, what would they do to *you* to get *me* to comply? The generals won't be with us for much longer—they'll be splitting off soon, leaving only me, and if Chen's men discover you can be used as leverage..."

"Keung," I whisper, tears in my eyes. I know I can't argue—he's right.

"I will hunt to the ends of the earth for you, Mulan—"

"But you're leaving me all the same."

His fingers are warm and rough as he wipes a tear from my cheek—the only one I'd allowed to escape.

"When the war is over—"

"There will *always* be a war, Keung," I interject. "There will always be something to fight."

He sighs. "You're right, Mulan. This isn't something I

can escape—there will always be wars to fight and having someone like you in my life is dangerous. You could always be used against me."

Keung sighs, hanging his head. "I just want you to be safe, even if it's not with me."

Even if we find the black jade blossom and return it to the emperor, Chen's men will keep coming for us. They've conquered Zhao Wu and usurped the emperor there—they need help restoring him to power. They've invaded other provinces. The armies of Yan Liu will always have battles to fight—perhaps Father was right when he told me I wasn't to marry a career soldier. A relationship with Keung can only end in a broken heart—we both know it. This hurts too much.

I pull away. If Keung wants to cut us off, I need to do it now before I dissolve into a teary mess.

"We can't have distractions while at war, Mulan. We can't!" he calls after me. I can hear the desperation in his voice. "I want to protect you."

"I can take care of myself." I wish he would trust me... trust *us*. I understand his point though—I can't trust us either right now.

A terrifying shriek fills the forest—a dragon.

Keung quickly overtakes me, rushing through the trees. He's elegant as he runs, nearly animal-like. I follow in his footsteps, hurrying to aid our men. We reach the end of the forest and he stops to look back for me.

"Go! I'll catch up. Go!" My words spur him on.

Instead of running, I slow, waiting near the end of the trees. When I'm sure he's not going to look back and I'm certain the soldiers are no longer at their posts near me, I shift.

Running, I move toward the camp and take off into the sky, beating my wings. I stifle my warrior cry, hoping my presence will be concealed until the last second.

When I arrive, dragons fill the air, roaring and screaming at each other. Our men have kept Chen's dragons at bay, refusing to let them reach the camp and set our supplies on fire as they try to keep us from their leader as he holds our life source captive.

I eye our dragons working in unison to fight against Chen's army. Their moves are nearly flawless—the communication techniques we were taught working magnificently. As I approach, I notice Chen's men doing the same.

My heart leaps—if we can learn how Chen's men communicate, we can know their moves before they strike during an attack.

I pull up, lifting higher into the air and dart around. Circling the outside of the fighting, I study what the dragons do. I note each move they execute, every noise, every dip in their motion, and commit each response to heart to tell Keung after the battle is quelled.

Jinhai sees me and calls to me. I shake my head in return—I'm not finished observing yet. He turns back to the battle, engaging with a dragon twice his size with claws far too long for its feet. He holds his own as Wei races to attack with him.

I turn back, watching Chen's army, searching for more signs of how they fight. I'm so focused on the battle in front of me, I'm shocked when a dragon latches onto my back and forces me toward the ground.

Chapter 9

Pain radiates from my lower back through my hips as he digs his claws into me. I shriek, reeling around to fight back. Pulling my wings close, I let him plummet us toward the earth.

My teeth sink into his foot, forcing him to release me, but he clings to me with the others. The dragon flaps his wings, slowing our descent. My claws lash out, swiping at him.

The true test of my capabilities is here—the jade dragon must be as powerful as it's supposed to be, or I'll be discovered for the fraud I am—or worse, not survive at all. If I fail now, Jinhai will pay the price, as will my family once the army returns—my father's title can't save them from this.

Should this army discover I am Mulan and not Lan, I will likely be tortured as the silver dragon woman was.

Her body was shredded last time I caught sight of her in the search for answers she refused to give up, scales marked onto her face to note her as an enemy in human form.

Wind rushes around me. I have to get this dark dragon off of me or I'll slam into the ground and die like the boy in the Center just days ago, barely able to return to my human form—if I die, maybe it's better if I stay the jade dragon to protect Jinhai. For that to work, though, Mulan will have to die too. When my body isn't found, Keung will search, so he says.

I hurl fire at the dark dragon, giving away the intensity of my blaze—my gift. Our dragons take notice—few men from Yan Lin have such powerful flames. I'll regret it later.

The dark dragon cries out as its scales start to melt under my fire. I knew my flame was strong, but I've never seen scales melt like that before—it's horrifying.

The dragon releases me, pawing at its face. My wings burst from my side and I pull myself out of the dive.

I've given away my secret; there's no point in hiding it now.

I strafe the line of dragons pushing our army back toward our camp. From above their line, I rain fire down on them, scorching their backs, but it doesn't stop them—

I'm too high up for it to damage them more than any other flame.

They shake their heads, lecturing me with their cries, but press forward, attacking our men. I turn, blasting them with my fire again to set them off balance. Without pausing, I dive straight down, colliding with the dragon who seems to be leading the attack.

He falters and one of our men assists me, slamming into his side. Wei appears, crashing into the dragon with his claws, sending him to the ground. The earth rumbles as he hits. Our men on the ground rush forward with their swords and take him out of the war.

I turn, looking above me as our army follows suit, attacking the scorched dragons. Racing up, I use my flames once more from the underside—the soft side—and surprise Chen's men.

After what surely must be an hour of excruciating battling, Chen's dragons retreat, leaving their dead mixed with ours on the ground.

I whip around searching for Jinhai in the air. When I find him next to Ning, my heart drops in relief only to panic again as I search for my red dragon lieutenant—even if he's no longer mine.

Jinhai calls to me, finally flying to my side, nudging me to fly away before I'm discovered. I can barely hold my head up, let alone fly. Without finding proof of Keung's safety, I take off to the trees with Jinhai next to me. He urges me on, forcing me not to go back.

I nearly crash into the trees as I land. Once on the ground, Jinhai blocks me from sight, allowing me to shift quickly before he does. I run into the woods before he loses the wings he has stretched out mightily to block my transformation.

He runs into the woods after me.

"Are you hurt?" My twin rushes to my side.

"They have a language," I inform him, one hand on my heart, trying to catch my breath, the other on a tree, attempting to hold myself upright.

"You exerted yourself more than any of us, Mulan, are you okay?" He grabs my wrist, pulling me away from the tree.

I fight to speak, air betraying my lungs. Every muscle screams. My limb feels detached. Searing pain rushes through my legs.

I claim to know Chen's language around Jinhai peppering me with questions about my sanity and comments about how the entire army knows of my strength now.

"What will you do when they put you on the front lines? How are we going to keep this a secret?"

My feet give out from under me. Jinhai scoops me into

his arms, rushing me toward the camp, but his movements are slow and unsteady from the fight.

I stop babbling about Chen's men long enough to beg Jinhai to put me down. "They can't see me like this—I'm Mulan—I was supposed to be helping the women and the wounded. I shouldn't be hurt like this."

My brother sets me on a rock and examines me.

"How are we supposed to survive this, Mulan?"

"What was I supposed to do, not help?" I counter, cringing as his fingers hit the mark on my outer hip where the dragon dug his claws into me for fun. I hiss at him. "I'm fine. I just need a minute."

My breath is ragged. I lean forward, resting on my knees. Breathing fire takes much out of a dragon but being attacked while flying is worse. The assault has left me struggling.

"What will we tell people?"

"That I was working, brother," I reply. "No one is going to ask about Mulan—they'll be too focused on Lan."

I rush to direct my brother. "Your time spent here in the trees was gathering information from him—from our *spy*. Keung informed people I was his contact today, so—"

"He did *what*?" Jinhai snaps. "Why was he even *near* you today?"

"I was called to assess the general after last night. He

wanted me to train afterward because he's worried about me—he doesn't know my secret."

Jinhai glares at me as I continue. "You can stop being so paranoid, he broke up with me."

"He did *what*?" he repeats his earlier question in the same livid tone. His expression morphs into the one he uses when he's upset for me.

"It's fine. He was right—it would be too easy to get caught. If Chen's men ever found out, it would be leverage against our commanding officer. And Father would kill me for—"

"Jinhai!" Wei's voice filters through the trees.

"Uh oh," my twin whispers. "Can you stand?"

"Yes." I clamber to my feet. I am a soldier.

"We're here!" I call out, trying to conceal my pain.

Wei and Ning burst through the trees. They look me over, assessing the situation.

"We know how Chen's army fights!" I call. "We need to speak to the generals."

"How did you manage this?" Daiyu asks, putting salve on my bloody hip.

It's quiet in the tent with just the two of us. Everyone

else is outside preparing to move again now that Chen's men know we're here.

"One of the fallen dragons got me when I was working. It's not a big deal."

"Your brother seems to think it is," she points out.

"Jinhai thinks *everything* is a big deal."

She makes a noise at the back of her throat and pushes her fingers into my side, making me jump. I clamp my teeth down, refusing to make a sound.

"Did I hear right about you being related to the jade dragon?" the medic asks. "I had heard rumors we had a spy in our midst—even that there was a secret, hidden man—but I didn't realize that was connected to *you*."

She wraps my waist, securing it in place. I sit when she's finished as she examines the rest of my body for injuries she needs to tend to.

"Yes, my brother."

"Your...*other* brother," she corrects me. "All done. Try not to get so scratched up next time, will you? I'm supposed to be helping the men, not the other medic."

"Sorry," I mumble, pulling my shirt back on. I stand and stride toward the door.

"*Mulan,*" she calls to me. "Be more careful next time —you don't know who is and isn't paying attention."

Turning her back on me, she dismisses me. I wonder if

she knows more than she's letting on—it almost sounded like a warning about my scales.

"Well?" Jinhai greets me outside the tent.

"I'm going to die. Say your goodbyes," I respond in a monotone voice, pushing past him.

"Good, do it on the intel mission," he replies.

"What?" I turn around.

"Your boyfriend has called for some of us to go on an intelligence-gathering expedition. *I* have to go, so *you* have to go."

"Why do *I* have to go? And he's not my *boyfriend*," I mutter.

"I'm not leaving you to your own devices around here. Last time I did that, you got slashed." Jinhai grabs my arm, spinning me around.

"How did we end up getting elected for this little mission?" I grumble, marching behind him. Most people ignore us as we hurry past them.

"I volunteered." His tone leaves no room for question.

"You did what?" I demand anyway.

"*Little pet!*" a tinkling voice calls. The silver dragon woman leans out of her cage, hands covered in knife marks. She beckons me as if she hadn't been tortured for information. "I see a destiny for you."

"Ignore her," Jinhai warns. "We're busy."

"I see your future, girl. I see it clearly as your love for—"

I turn, silencing her. Walking the distance between us, I seethe as I draw near.

"What do you want, silver dragon?"

"Our destinies are intertwined, little pet. I see that now." She reaches for me, but I keep out of her grasp. "Your past was so pretty; your future will be brilliant. It will dazzle in the firelight in the palace of the emperor. *You and I* shall sit there with his highness and *reign*."

"I *hardly* think the emperor will allow you to live, witch."

"*Witch?*" she scoffs. "No. It's my dragon gift—the gift of sight. Surely your handsome man here has a gift—all dragons do...some more intently than others."

Jinhai's gift was given to me. He makes up for it with his ability to outthink others, but I don't tell her that.

"I see it so clearly, little pet. One day, you'll see him and revel in his beauty as I do—as we all do." The silver dragon sits up in her cage. "Help me escape, dear, and I'll take you to him to rule by his side. He told me he's waiting for you."

"The mad ramblings of a captive waiting to be executed," her guard mumbles. "Ignore her."

"Are they executing her?" I question.

"That's the word going around, but no one has given the order yet," he replies.

Jinhai grunts to the man with a nod and turns us to go. "We have more important things, Mulan."

The woman reaches out and brushes a single finger against my arm—I have no idea how she reached me.

"See you soon, *little pet.*"

I claw at her, smacking her hand away from me. The guard forces her back, beating on the bars with his open palm in an attempt to redirect her attention off me.

The party consists of ten soldiers including me and my brother. Wei and Ning walk with us. I avoid speaking to Ning as we walk, still angry he ran to my brother about Keung—I knew he wouldn't keep it from him. He watches me out of the corner of his eye, waiting for me to forgive him.

The stench of smoke fills the air even as we get farther away from the campsite. The group intends to meet us at the next location so Chen's men can't find them—we're just taking the long way there.

"What are we looking for exactly?" one of the soldiers asks.

"Signs of rebels," another answers. "Our spies. A dragon that needs beheading. Take your pick."

"We need a better view," Jinhai announces. "Mulan?"

I sigh, walking toward a nearby tree. My brother boosts me up and I climb as high as I feel the tree can hold me. My uniform is helpful for the climb, but I still miss my kimonos. I'd trade my next meal to be able to wear my pink dress for a few hours.

"Looks like there's a path to the left," I call down. "I assume it leads to a village."

"We should check it out," Wei says when I drop out of the tree. He grabs my hand before Jinhai can, steadying me.

The leader angles us in the direction of the path. I stay quiet as the boys talk. Eventually, the conversation steers toward women. I put in my opinions on girls back home who might date Wei and Ning.

"What about that Liling girl, Jinhai? She seems awfully taken with you." Wei elbows my brother.

I roll my eyes and stifle a comment. The birds chatter at them for me, but the boys ignore the calls.

"We had a nice conversation earlier," Jinhai breezily replies, catching my full attention.

"You're flirting with that child?" My voice is more clipped than I mean it to be, earning me a look.

"You're one to judge, sis. And she's not that much younger."

"Young enough..."

"Do you two want us to step out so you can have this sibling squabble, or...?" Wei jokes.

"I think we need to find the black jade blossom just to bring Jinhai's love life back to life," Ning jumps in on the harassment. "He hasn't dated since—"

"Just because I don't consistently spend time with one woman doesn't mean I'm not seeing women," Jinhai says sharply. Getting my brother to commit has always been a task.

The three harass each other, laughing quietly. I envy their comradery. I was friendly with girls in the village, but my brother is the only one I ever truly considered a friend...or at least, a friendship that lasted.

I tune them out, letting them have their fun while I listen for sounds in the distance. It's quiet. The smell of smoke drifts by, reminding us even in our solitude, we're not safe.

The path seems isolated when we reach it. It winds down through the sparse trees, guiding us toward an unseen village. We quiet as our surroundings indicate we're close enough that we should be careful.

A wall divides the field in front of us, acting as a gate barrier to the village. When our leader cautiously works his way around the corner, peeking around the rock, he gasps and waves us forward.

Stepping through, we see the entire village glowing red as it smolders, embers and ashes licking up toward the late afternoon sky.

Chapter 10

Bodies bleed in the streets. Some burn in the rubble of destroyed buildings. Dragon carcasses form massive mountains that block our way as we rush forward to look for survivors.

Heads have been decapitated from bodies. Others have been slashed or burned, charred beyond recognition.

A dragon cries out in pain so softly that it's silenced before it can finish, eyes closing. Fire crackles around it, snapping and hissing.

My body betrays me, shaking in horror. I jump as a building behind us collapses under the flames' damage.

"Is anyone alive?" our leader calls. He turns to us. "I don't see anyone but be careful. The enemy should be long gone, but if anyone is hiding here, we must be on our guard.

"Spread out." He pairs us up, sending us to search for anything we can salvage and take back.

"Are you okay?" Wei asks quietly, staying close.

"This is awful," I reply softly. Kicking some boards with my boot, I uncover more charred supplies that we can no longer use.

Wei looks over a group of bodies too far gone to even check for a pulse. "They destroyed everything. How could they have even possibly done this?"

"It looks mainly like warriors and dragons here—at least they got the villagers to safety before they struck. The weyr fought valiantly, even if they were overtaken." I cough as smoke fills my lungs.

"Over here!" Ning calls.

We all turn to see what he's pointing at. He tugs at boards that somehow missed the flames.

"Something moved." I gasp.

Racing over, we're the last group to arrive to aid Ning. A new man trips, falling to his knees as he coughs. Rising up, he drags himself up on the pile of boards.

His chest rises and falls heavily as he struggles to catch his breath. He's wearing our colors—he's one of us. Ning supports him, helping him walk over to us.

"Please." He coughs again. "Help."

One of the men holds a sword to him. "Careful."

"Get back, solider, we don't know him," the lieutenant

traveling with us orders Ning to move. He immediately does, leaving the man standing.

"I'm one of you," the man insists, standing on his own finally. He reaches up, brushing back his short black hair.

Something ticks in the back of my mind—something familiar.

"*Xun?*" Jinhai figures it out first. The man's head snaps up, connecting with my brother.

My lungs fill with a sharp burst of air. I squint, trying to see if it's the same boy from my childhood. The hair is right...so are his eyes.

"Jinhai." He breathes.

It's him—the boy I met while he was traveling with his father. They're merchants, like us, only their dealings lead them to travel far more than father ever did. They stayed for a week or two at a time before moving on but passed through maybe four or five times as I was growing up. He was a charmer if I recall.

"Xun?" I wait to see if he reacts to me. His gaze swings over, eyes opening in shock. After a moment, he grins. *It's definitely him.*

"Well, if it isn't Lin Mulan, the prettiest girl in all of Yan Liu." He coughs, ruining his suave greeting. It looks like he wants to run over and hug me, but he restrains himself. "I believe the Lin siblings can vouch for me."

"He's one of us," Jinhai assures them. "We knew him growing up."

Ning attempts to help Xun walk, but the now-grown man waves him off, walking to us himself. He claps Jinhai on the shoulder in greeting and bows deeply to me.

"What happened here, Xun?" Jinhai asks.

"The village burned. We weren't ready for the strike." He describes the bloody battle. I notice the marks on his face that will thankfully heal. His clothing is torn but will suffice until we meet the rest of our army. "We were passing through to meet with...I assume *you*...when they attacked."

"You're the sole survivor," I say quietly. He turns to look at me as we walk. His lips twitch but he doesn't address me.

"They brought honor to Yan Liu." His words leave a heavy feeling over the group.

Without giving away details of our mission or information about our location, the men inform my childhood friend that we're meeting the rest of the soldiers by nightfall. It's strange seeing him again after all these years. I had forgotten about him until Jinhai said his name.

The colors fade around us as the light dwindles. I long for a loaf of bread to eat—I haven't stopped to eat since the attack—but it will have to wait until we find the camp.

We walk together in silence, knowing we can't speak

with Xun until the general approves him to join our army. Xun describes more of the battle for us, filling the empty space, but eventually falls silent too.

He looks over his shoulder at me as we walk from time to time, offering me a weak smile. Once he's been presented to the general, I'm sure we'll catch up. I'm anxious to see what his life has been like since I last saw him many years ago.

Eventually, we find the spies left to wait for us and follow them back to the campsite. It glows orange with fire and smoke, this time, the kind from campfires.

We're guided to the meeting tent where the generals and lieutenants are waiting for us. The team waits outside while our leader takes Xun inside. After a few moments, Jinhai and I are waved forward.

It's warm inside the tent and smells delightfully of food. My stomach rumbles against my will and Keung glances over at me.

You'll eat in a few minutes, I remind myself.

"You know Tang Xun?" the general asks.

"Yes, sir. He and his father were merchants and traveled to some of the same locations our father traveled after his retirement," Jinhai answers, bowing respectfully. I nod.

"Very well. He may be permitted to join us. Please see that he gets a new uniform and send that damaged one to the girl to be mended," the general directs one of his men.

The man bows and motions for Xun to follow him. Xun bows to the general.

"Tang Xun," the general stops him as he turns to leave. "This is your lieutenant general and commanding officer, Yu Keung. You will follow his orders as I prepare to leave."

Xun nods and leaves the tent.

So, the general is finally splitting off from us.

"Thank you for your work today," the general says. "You are dismissed."

Keung doesn't look at me as I turn to go. He's really holding to this ridiculous idea. I should be too—I can never be with him, not really. We duck out of the tent without looking back.

"We should find him," I comment. Jinhai nods and we set off to look for Xun.

The stars sparkle in the evening sky which hasn't faded from navy to black yet. The moon rests in the corner, still full and brilliant, but covered by clouds.

"Ah, we'll take him," Jinhai calls, noticing Xun being led to a fire. The men nod and leave Xun to be shown around by us.

"My old friends," Xun says, grinning as we approach.

We find a place with Ning and Wei by a fire. Wei

hands me bread and I fight not to devour it. Slowly, I pick it apart and eat it.

"Where have you been all these years, Xun?" Jinhai asks, handing him food.

"Traveling the province, mostly. Work has been good, so we haven't traveled as much."

"No wonder we haven't seen you," Jinhai replies. "How is your father?"

"Fine last I saw him. Yours?"

"Well, thank you," Jinhai informs him.

"You had a kid sister last I saw you, isn't that right?" Xun closes his eyes as he tastes the bread. Reaching out, he accepts a bowl of stew from Ning. The scent wafts over to me and I eagerly wait for Ning to hand one to me.

"She's grown now." My brother nods.

"As beautiful as your sister here?" Xun grins and looks at me, throwing me off as I focus on how warm the fire is making my toes. I suck in a breath and hold his gaze.

"War is no place for courtships, Xun," Jinhai warns.

"Of course not, my friend. I've always said your sister was beautiful—please don't feel like you need to watch out for me—I'll be respectful, won't I, Mulan?" Xun swings his gaze back over to me.

We both know he put a flower in my hair the last time we saw each other, but neither of us will admit to that. We were far too young to court then, but our easy friendship seems like it hasn't missed a beat.

"Jinhai, leave him alone. You know he's nothing to worry about."

The stew tastes amazing—I'll have to let Liling know next time I see her. It *must* be good if I'm willing to compliment her. I savor the stew's warmth as it fills me.

The men chat while I focus on eating. Eventually, they get up to move, taking the bowls back. Our seating arrangements shift and Xun slides over next to me while the others are lost in conversation about the women they're interested in again.

"So," he starts, bumping into my shoulder. "It's been a long time."

"It has." I smile.

"How have things *really* been?" He asks, nodding to my brother.

"We've been fine." I fall back into our old way of conversation as if I'd seen him last week instead of years ago. "Mother is still as strong as ever. Father's injury is giving him some trouble, but he's navigating things anyway. You'd love my little sister, Ming—she's a troublemaker."

Xun chuckles. "Sounds like I would. And you, Mulan? What have you been doing all these years?"

"Training and working with my father, mostly."

"Still selling tea then. How charming." He smiles warmly. "It sounds like you've made a lovely life for yourself. Any husband?"

"No." I smile, embarrassed. "Nothing like that. I have too much to do to help father, especially since Jinhai was supposed to be going off to war."

"Yes, how *did* you end up here, Mulan? Two dragons from the same family certainly can't be part of the conscription mandate."

I elbow him harshly. "*No one can know about that, Xun.*" My harsh whisper surprises him and his eyes widen, pulling back his ears and tightening his skin around his lips.

"Know—?" He pauses before whispering in a hiss. "*Wait, they don't know you're a dragon?*"

"No, now be quiet!" terror runs through me. *They can't find out I'm a dragon.*

Xun leans into me, ensuring no one overhears us. His shoulder feels strong against mine—he's acquired more muscle since the last time I saw him.

"I won't tell anyone, but *surely* they can't hold that against you, Mulan. You grew up in Yan Liu. You're a daughter of the province."

"My scales must remain a secret, Xun, please."

His little finger grazes over the back of my hand. "Your secret is safe with me, my friend."

Ning falls hard, dropping his bo staff. The circle claps, making jokes at his expense. He stands, bowing to me, accepting his defeat.

"I'll keep quiet next time, *sheesh*," he mumbles, rising.

At least I know how to threaten him the next time he catches me doing something I shouldn't.

"Who's next?" Keung asks, walking the outside of the circle as he inspects our training group.

"I am!" Jinhai announces. He nods for me to step back in.

Everyone takes a step back, knowing the sibling rivalry will be less controlled than the other spars. Xun, Ning, and Wei all rock back on their feet, waiting for the show.

My twin waits for me to strike first. I oblige, taunting him under my breath as our bo staffs collide. We take it seriously at first, knowing everyone is watching, but it quickly gets out of hand. Men jump back as we nearly crash into them. I run for the nearby tree, knowing the group will move out of my way.

Xun yells to me from the outside of the circle, cheering me on, while Ning stands decidedly with Jinhai in the fight after I defeated him in the last match. Wei cheers, diplomatically refusing to use any names, but the rest of the men pick a side, calling to us to take the other out.

I push off of the tree, swinging my weapon at my brother. He blocks and tries to hit me mid-air. When I land, I go for his feet, narrowly ducking the blow to my head.

"Is that the best you've got, Mulan? You must be tired from your last fight!" Jinhai calls.

"Just getting warmed up," I reply, twirling the bo staff in my hand. When it stops, I grasp it and get down to business.

We're so loud and rambunctious, two other groups stop to watch us. For a minute, I forget we're at war instead of sparring in the field outside our family home in the village. There's nothing here but me and my brother trying to best each other and a few of our friends cheering us on.

The battle continues and I lose my breath, but Jinhai is still holding strong. If I have to lose to him, I'll hold it off as long as possible.

Glancing up, I quickly catch sight of the excited faces around us watching the fun. For the moment, we're a distraction, which, I'm sure, is the only reason we haven't been stopped yet and told to focus on real training.

"Destroy him, Mulan!" Xun's voice filters above the crowd.

I deliver a powerful blow that nearly knocks Jinhai to the ground. He uses the opportunity to pull my ankle out with the end of his staff and sends me toppling down instead, ending the match.

My brother walks over and helps me up. I rub my hip where the skin throbs from the collision with the ground, still sore from the dragon attack. It's going to be sore tomorrow, especially after sleeping on it.

"Mulan, that was fantastic!" Xun runs over and throws an arm around me. "I always knew you could handle yourself, but you really grew into your own these last few years."

I grin, pleased I could impress my old friend. He stands beside me, arm over my shoulder as he banters with my brother. From the corner of my eye, I see Keung mumbling and staring at us.

"That was incredible!" Xun announces again as if he hadn't just spent a full minute telling us how epic our battle was.

"It would have been more impressive if they had taken it seriously," Keung snips. He raises his voice and shouts, "Back to training!"

Jinhai glances at him. He pulls away and walks toward our commanding officer. Brushing past me, he whispers, "Great, you made him mad. Now I have to fix this."

I turn, slipping out from under Xun's arm to glare at my brother, but he can't see me as he walks toward the lieutenant. I can hear him trying to buddy up with Keung, much to my shock. After a few minutes, I turn back around to look at them, but Keung only looks away, leaving me unsure of where we stand.

Xun steps into the circle for his first spar. One of the other soldiers steps in with him and the two begin to attack. I watch quietly, not wanting to cause any more distractions.

"So, what do we really think of him?" Ning asks quietly from a few feet away. They always forget I have exceptional hearing.

"Jinhai likes him, so I guess that means we do too," Wei answers.

The men in the circle illicit a cheer from the crowd and I realize I stopped watching the match. I drop my eyes to the ground where their feet move gracefully as they spar and focus my attention on the conversation next to me.

"He seems awfully close to Mulan. Should we be worried—especially after I caught her with the lieutenant?"

"Mulan is a big girl, she can take care of herself," Wei chastises, making me approve more of his friendship with my brother. "That said, Jinhai doesn't like it, but he approves of it more than the lieutenant. He said something about not trusting the 'guy groping his sister in the marketplace'."

I tip my hair down, trying to hide the blush I know has raced to my cheeks. The next time my brother and I spar, I'm going to give him a concussion for this.

"Is that why he ran over there after the match? To tell him to back off?"

"He can't tell his commanding officer to back off, Ning." Wei pauses. "He's been shooting icy daggers at him this whole time though. It looks like the lieutenant has backed off."

"There's nothing going on," I turn and whisper harshly. "You can stop."

Both boys turn, embarrassment tinging their cheeks red. They mumble apologies and turn away.

"Does he want us to watch out for her?" Ning whispers, still loud enough for me to hear.

I sigh loudly and turn to walk away as a loud cheer fills the air behind me. The match must have ended.

After a moment, footsteps run up to me. A hand touches my shoulder, slowing me as I hurry toward the women's tent to escape my brother and his overprotective friends.

"Let's take a walk," Xun says, steering me in the opposite direction.

Chapter 11

"This is such a beautiful area," I comment, walking behind the rest of the scouting team.

"It is," Xun agrees. "It's nice to get out of the camp."

"Yeah, it was starting to get stifling in there."

He reaches up, brushing his hair out of his eyes. "Must be hard being one of the only women."

We're far enough away from the other men that they can't hear us talk as we walk through the abandoned town. Many of the outer villages fled when the Zhao Wu soldiers started infiltrating our borders to take the black jade blossom from us.

"You really hold your own, though."

"Years of practice," I reply. "Are you finding your way?"

"Oh, yes." Xun offers me a smile. "Everything has

been *very* informative. I've learned a lot since joining you all."

"Since last night?" I giggle.

"Yes." He chuckles too. "I can't wait to tell my father what I've learned in this short time."

I start to say something, but he cuts me off, changing the subject as the trees rustle in the wind around us.

"I'm so glad I found you and your brother again, Mulan. Something just *told* me I'd see you once more." He brushes into me, knocking my shoulder playfully. "It's been far too long. I've missed your spirit."

"I've missed you too, Xun. I—"

I stop as our team leader holds up his hand for silence. Next to me, Xun tenses, placing a hand on his sword. My fingers make their way to my own weapon and I lower my stance, prepared to strike should we have stumbled upon the enemy.

Unlike our battles in the woods or meadows, we're surrounded by buildings. The streets were once filled with people, but now only contain the remnants of a life given up. Carts lay in the roads where their merchants left them, goods still sitting in the open—at least what looters didn't take.

Xun takes a step closer to me and it almost feels like we have the same connection I do with my brother—we know each other's moves even from so long ago. We'll be able to work together without trouble.

Silence stretches out, trying to lull us into relaxing, but something isn't right. The air is stiff; it crackles with tension—someone is here watching us.

No one moves, waiting. We watch the buildings, staring at entrances and windows, looking for some sign of the enemy. They're here—we're certain of it—we just don't know where.

My breath is heavy, filling my lungs and expanding my chest as I focus intently on finding Chen's men. I want to draw my sword, but any movement could set off a chain reaction, so I wait until I'm sure.

Xun's arm against mine is comforting...until he removes it. He draws his sword, and everyone follows suit.

The first enemy soldier appears, running silently at one of our men in the front. Another steps out of a doorway and approaches us.

With sword in hand, I prepare to fight. I'm thankful I tied my hair back before we left, making it easier for me to see as I swing around and protect myself, sword clashing loudly against the enemy's. I wish I could use my bow, but I'm far too close for that.

"Lin!" Xun shouts to me, wisely avoiding my first name.

I turn, blocking an oncoming sword just in time.

Reaching down, I cut the back of his ankle and the man screams. Xun hurries to my side, killing the man.

"Hurry," Xun says, pulling me down the stone path. We race past buildings as Chen's men chase us.

As we run, I hear the sound of footsteps, and worse, the sound of hooves racing across the stone path. The man and his horse overtake us, trying to force us onto an isolated side street.

Xun grabs my arm, tugging me along. We duck into a house and rush to the opposite door in hopes of escape but the soldier on the horse nearly collides with us as we exit.

My friend throws me against a wall, trying to protect me, but he leaves his back open for attack. The horseman rides up to us, ready to stab Xun, but I move first, thrusting my sword into his side from around my friend. He wobbles, dazed that he was struck. Xun turns and pushes him off the horse.

The man falls to the ground as we rush around the animal. Xun launches himself onto the horse's back while I reach down and take the man's weapon. My friend reaches down for me. I grab his hand and allow him to pull me up.

More men on horses enter the mouth of the street. Noticing us, they gallop toward us. Xun and I kick our mount at the same time, sending him racing forward through the abandoned street.

Xun takes us back toward the skirmish. I watch our backs as he guides us. The men get close enough for me to attempt to reach, but my arms just aren't long enough to stab them. Instead, I block their blades, protecting Xun as he handles the reigns.

"Careful!" Xun yells. One hand moves back to me, grabbing my leg as if to steady me.

"I've got this, just get us out of here!" I shout back, using my knees to clamp onto the horse so I don't fall off.

"Hold on to me!" he cautions.

"I need both hands, I'm fine," I reply, gripping tighter with my legs.

The wind whips against my face as we charge ahead, slowing only to take corners. The buildings fly past me in a blur.

"Hold me *now!*" Xun screams, changing his tone. He trusted me enough to ride behind him without holding on for this long, so he must have a plan.

Twisting the swords around and tucking them in, I wrap my arms around Xun's waist tightly and he immediately brings the horse to a stop. Chen's men continue to fly past us giving us an opportunity to wheel around and turn down another street.

When we find the main skirmish, we've lost several of our men, and what appears to be several of Chen's men. I leap off of the horse and pull out both swords to fight with. Xun remains on the horse, brandishing his sword as well.

The fighting continues, leaving blood in the streets. A soldier slices my arm, tearing my skin sharply. He kicks out my foot with his, sending me toppling to the ground. I consider kicking his foot out as well, but as he closes in with sword drawn high, I do the only thing I can think of —swing my sword at his ankle. He falls, leg no longer attached to his foot.

Horror washes over me. The blood pools out of his leg, filling the cracks in the stone path in an intricate design. I scramble up, moving away. My body reacts violently, not allowing me to kill the enemy as I know I should. I shudder.

Pulling back, I engage with another man, battling until one of the other soldiers stabs him in the side for me. I nod my thanks.

Xun's yell grabs my attention. A soldier pulls him off the horse and pins him against a building.

The riderless horse slows at it reaches me and I manage to grab the reins. Lifting myself up, I race toward Xun. I kick the enemy's head so hard as I rush past that he collapses on the ground and doesn't move. Xun looks impressed.

One of Chen's men finds room to transform and shifts

into his dragon form. On the horse, I'm an easy target, so I quickly dismount and run for cover.

Out of breath, I huddle in the corner of an open house. The dragon roars outside, setting flames to what I hope is a building and not one of my team members.

The dragon moves away and the world quiets. Suddenly, something catches my eye across the dark, empty house. A figure rises and moves toward me.

"What do we have here?"

He reaches me before I can pull out my weapon. The man drops to his knees, pinning me against the wall. I kick out, but he has the advantage with his size and strength—I should have been more prepared for this.

"Quiet, girl!" he growls, leaning in. "Cooperate and I'll take you to Chen instead of killing you. He'd like a concubine like you around."

The man eyes me, dragging his gaze over my folded form. Jerking my wrists together, he pins them above my head. I twist, trying to free myself as he reaches for cords to bind me. "I'll be rewarded handsomely for you, girl."

I scream, hoping someone will hear me. I'd even be willing for the dragon's help at this point, despite it meaning my death. He binds me quickly, ensuring I can't shift even if I tried.

"Get off of me!" I attempt to kick again, but he uses his knee to slam into my side, crumpling me to the side into his knee. One hand rakes down my shoulder, clawing at me painfully.

The man's piercing nails dig into my side as he tries to flip me to bind my legs so I can't run when he carries me out of the house. A dark figure walks up behind him, ready to assist.

The person nearly growls as he approaches, stalking up to us. Every muscle is taught, strained with each step as he looks like he tries to control his movements. His hand reaches out, clamping down on the man.

On my stomach, I watch him from the corner of my eye over my shoulder as I continue to struggle. His hand finds its way to my captor's shoulder and roughly wrenches it back. The man falls, releasing me.

"*You* do not touch her." Xun towers over him terrifyingly.

I flip over and scoot back, hands still bound. I press myself up against the house wall, righting myself and preparing to run as I watch Xun pull a blade from his belt and slowly plunge it into my captor's heart.

"*You* do not touch her," Xun repeats, seething.

The man falls to the ground slowly. His blood trickles out onto the ground and makes its way to me.

"Get up," Xun whispers harshly, not taking his eyes off the dying man.

I scramble to my feet, wide-eyed, and rush to his side.

He snaps out of it after a moment and wraps his arm around me, pulling me to his side. Pulling his eyes away from the man bubbling blood from his lips, Xun rushes us toward the door.

Outside, two of our men lay in the street, dead. Their throats had been cut, leaving them bleeding helplessly just feet away from me as I was being attacked. Xun guides me around them, ensuring I don't trip over their bodies.

Together, we run down the streets. At some point, he had his shirt ripped open and one side hangs loosely, flapping behind him as we run. He punches a soldier who runs at us, protecting me, but he doesn't stop our flight.

I follow his commands as he pushes me through alleyways and around corners. My wrists ache from being bound so tightly and I worry about my circulation being cut off.

Finally, he stops us, coming to a nearly fatal halt inside a jade palace. We slide, nearly dropping, but jerk to a stop.

"Here," he says harshly, pulling me to a low wall meant only to act as décor inside the main room of the jade palace. Xun forces me to sit and takes a seat beside me. "We're safe. Give me your hands."

I breathe so hard my entire body is shaking. I offer

him my hands, but he only stares at them as he silently slides his free hand up my wrist over the bindings.

"Slow your breath, Mulan."

Immediately, I breathe out, forcing myself to calm my intake of air. It hurts my lungs to not get the air I need, but I also know Xun can't cut off the bindings if he might cut my wrist open in the process if I jerk my hands under his grasp with my wild breathing.

Carefully, he slides his blade under the bindings and frees me. I pull my elbows back, resting my wrists on my knees. I take turns using one hand to massage my wrists, encouraging the blood flow as Xun watches me.

"Where are we?" I ask, breaking the silence.

"A jade palace," he replies. "We're safe here. Are you alright?"

I inhale a deep breath and nod. Glancing around, I take in the marble look of the palace, green filling the space. It must have been brilliant in its day.

"You were terrifying back there," I comment.

"I was *trying* to be." His smirk makes me roll my eyes. "You weren't too bad yourself with that horse back there."

He reaches out, running his fingers over the injuries on my shoulders and arm. Quietly, he rips a strip from his open shirt and bandages the worst of the cuts on my upper arm.

"We'll be a sight when we get back," he jokes.

I appraise the wounds on this chest—all superficial, thankfully.

"Are you hurt?" I ask, pulling back his ripped shirt to reveal his chiseled stomach.

Xun watches me closely as I examine him, one hand still in his. I absent-mindedly stare. His lips make a slight popping sound as they separate, his gaze locked on my face, but I refuse to look at him as he hovers near me.

With his free hand, Xun reaches for mine and places my fingertips on his chest, surprising me. He lightly traces it along his body until my hand rests on his shoulder.

I swallow, still refusing to look at him. My breathing slows—everything slows. When I was a girl, I thought this day might come, but now that it has, I'm surprised.

I pull in my bottom lip, trying to decide what to do as his eyes pierce through me.

Chapter 12

Xun tastes like fire burning through me. His lips are insatiable, roaming over my shoulders and jaw. I wrap my hands around his neck, pulling him close.

My forearms rest against his bare chest and I'm acutely aware of his skin against mine. The child version of me who called Xun a friend would never have imagined this moment like this—at least, not this passionately.

Xun lifts me up, pulling me onto his lap. My legs dangle over the edge of the wall, too high to reach the ground now.

"I won't let them touch you," Xun murmurs into my skin as he kisses my shoulder.

His hands tangle in my hair. I forget the jade palace. I forget the war. I forget the way Keung turned me away.

Xun's laugh pulls me out of my trance. When I look up, his face radiates pure joy.

"I've been waiting years to finally be with you again." His satisfied grin makes me smile back.

"You didn't kiss me like that last time," I remind him.

"We were kids," he jokes. "We couldn't have done that back then."

Maybe this is the way it's supposed to be. Xun has always intended to follow in his father's footsteps—he's not here by choice. A life with someone like him is the one I've always been destined for. Xun makes sense for me.

"Well, lucky us, all grown up."

"Lucky us, just old enough to fight in the war." He means me—he's a few years older, but had I not just turned eighteen, Jinhai would never have been called and I would never have been in the Center during the attack.

He kisses me again, lighter this time.

"And now that I have you, I'm not letting you go, Mulan. I've waited far too long for this moment. I'll take you away from this war, I promise. I'll give you everything and turn you into the princess you deserve to be."

I giggle. Xun always had dreams of grandeur, talking of palaces and wealth and glory.

I lean in and rest against him. Keung flashes in my mind, but I have to remind myself that he's the one who stopped us from being together. It was his decision to let me go—even if it was to keep me safe—so I'm not doing anything wrong by kissing my childhood best friend.

"I miss your pretty kimonos, Mulan," he murmurs. "Not that you don't look radiant—*you do*, my warrior queen—but there's something about that pink kimono you used to wear."

"The one with the red and purple detailing on it?" I'm surprised he remembered.

"Yes. You used to wear your hair up so fancy with that."

"The *one* time you saw me in it," I remind him, brushing his hair out of his face.

"Don't fault me for being dragged away to work with my father," he quips. "If I could have brought you along with me that day, I would have."

Xun nuzzles against me. "I've missed you more than you can know."

"I didn't realize how much I missed you," I reply. It's been lonely.

I trail my hand up and down Xun's arm without thinking. It's amazing how easily we've come back together.

Drawings of dragons fill the walls etched in gold. The screens are covered in dust but appear to have escaped any signs of damage since their abandonment. Silks hang from the ceiling, draping quietly in the corners.

"We should go," Xun murmurs after a few minutes. "This is not the palace I promised you, so if I'm going to keep my word, we need to get moving."

He waits for me to stand, releasing him. I turn and hold my hand to Xun and pull him up from the top of the short jade wall.

My legs are unsteady, so Xun dips under my arm and wraps himself around my back to support me. I give in, leaning against him more for comfort than actual need of his support.

Outside, we pass the pool of water next to the palace. Intricate designs fill the outside walls of the palace in red, blue, and yellow hues. Dragon statues sit on either side of the palace, greeting visitors and guarding against unwanted forces.

We walk through the isolated village, leaving the jade palace behind. No enemy army greets us. No dragons fly in our wake. We're safe for the time.

Together, we make our way past houses with curved up roofs, lanterns still dangling in the breeze. Dragon detailing can be found everywhere I look—much more than we have back home near the emperor's palace.

"There you are!" A man says. Turning, he yells, "They're here!"

Men come running around the corner as we step onto the path that brought us to the village. Jinhai nearly crumbles in relief. He rushes to me.

"What happened?" His voice comes out as a gasp. "Are you okay?"

My brother pulls me away from Xun, drawing me in for a painful hug.

"Careful," I chastise. "We're fine."

Jinhai pulls back and examines me, noting every scrape and cut. His eyes grow wide when he notices the marks from the bindings, but they quickly narrow as he looks up to glare at me, demanding an answer. I give a single, quick shake of my head to warn him off. He holds his tongue, but turns us, tucking me to his side, and motions for us to start back to the camp.

"Are you okay, Xun?" He asks, keeping up appearances as we walk. Slowing our pace, he puts space between us and the other men who came to help the survivors of the skirmish. Our friends hold back, eager to find out what happened after hearing what I'm sure were horrifying stories from the other men that were in the village with us.

"A man cornered me," I admit quietly when I'm sure I can't be overheard. "I didn't know he was in the house."

I can feel the anger radiating off Jinhai, Wei, and Ning next to me. Xun walks quietly behind, letting them stand guard over me.

"He held me down before I could defend myself and managed to bind my hands. Xun showed up and rescued me." I leave out the details to spare my brother worry.

"He's dead," Xun mumbles in that same terrifying

voice he used with the man before he killed him. "You don't have to worry about him."

Jinhai looks back over his shoulder between us. He nods to Xun.

"You would have been impressed with her—she saved me, too," Xun admits, voice lighter. "Took a guy out with a boot to the head while on horseback. It was quite the sight."

Jinhai snorts, unable to hold back his laugh. Then he laughs for real, letting go of his stress over the situation. Wei and Ning join him before Xun and I follow in as well. The relief is overwhelming as it washes my tension away like a good bath does.

I stretch my far arm back, reaching for Xun's hand. Jinhai feels the movement under my shoulder and traces it back to where Xun has grasped my fingers tenderly. My brother clamps his jaw down but doesn't say anything —I've won.

Keung breathes a deep sigh of relief when his team of men discovers us in the woods. He hurries over to get a report. The men fill him in, and he listens intently to their descriptions of the fight.

"Sir," one of our spies addresses our leader. "We

should leave quickly. At least some of the rebels made it out alive which means they're likely looking for us with reinforcements."

"I agree." Keung nods. "It's time to move. It will be dark soon enough. Go tell the others we're leaving."

I drop Xun's hand when Keung looks over at me. He might have broken things off, but we were together what feels like only moments ago—I want to be respectful of him.

He squints at Xun, offering him an icy stare. I'm impressed it's not a glare. The lieutenant's hand twitches at his side and I can tell he's trying not to ball it into a fist. He glances back at me, this time assessing my injuries.

"You should have that looked at before we go," he addresses me as he walks by. "Have your brother take you."

Jinhai snaps his head in our direction and moves to my side. "I'll take her."

I'm not sure if my injuries are any worse than Xun's or any of the other men's, but I play along, not wanting to agitate the situation. I cast one last look over my shoulder at Xun as Jinhai leads me away.

"Congratulations, you've managed to upset your boyfriend and then *really* upset him by parading your *new* boyfriend in front of him," Jinhai announces when we're far enough away from everyone.

"I'm not trying to upset Keung." I sigh. "He's the one who broke it off with me."

"Want me to kill him for you?" Jinhai asks seriously.

"No." I glance at him quickly. He's definitely serious. "He just wanted to keep me safe and make sure Chen's men can't use me as leverage...which I get...but it still really hurts."

"And your solution is to run into the arms of another man?" My brother's bluntness is part of his charm.

"I didn't mean for that to happen either." I blink. It's been a whirlwind of a week. First, I was practically promised an engagement from Keung, then he leaves me. Then Xun shows up and claims me in a relationship—although, is it? We haven't discussed anything beyond that kiss, aside from his princess comment.

"If both options were available to you, which would you choose?" Jinhai glances at me. "I want to make sure you're with Xun for the right reasons."

"You think I'm kissing Xun because I'm upset at Keung?"

Jinhai blanches when I confirm I've kissed Xun. He nearly looks like he's going to be sick.

"While I'd vastly prefer Xun over that pretentious guy you nursed back to health in secret, I don't think you should be with him if it's simply because you're still raw from the way you left things with the lieutenant." He pauses. "But I'm still pulling for Xun."

"What *is* your issue with Keung?" I ask as we duck under a rope tethered from one tent to another.

"We'll come back to that," he mutters. "We're here. Come find me when you're done. You're still traveling with me when we move out."

Jinhai steps back to leave, motioning that he's watching me. I chuckle under my breath as I turn to find Song stepping out of our tent as if she were expecting me. Her eyes are big and bright as she takes me in.

"We're going to have to fix that." She motions to me, turning to call back into the tent. "Daiyu! Mulan is back and needs your attention!"

I step into the tent, instantly feeling warmer. Everything is sitting in a pile by the door waiting to be tied onto a dragon's back.

"What do we have here?" Daiyu asks, wiping her hands on a rag.

"Spy mission gone wrong?" I ask as if it's a question. I shrug but instantly regret it as a stinging sensation crawls through my left shoulder.

"Take it off and let me fix it," Song commands. Her voice is still soft, but the gentleness is gone as she adopts a professional tone. She hands me a kimono to wear while she sews up my uniform.

Daiyu checks me over, putting salve on my injuries. Before she allows me to stand up, she pushes a small bottle into my hands. "Here, take this, you're going to need it before you shift."

"What?" I gape at her.

"Don't give me that look, Mulan, I know a dragon when I see one."

"But I'm not—" I try to protest.

"I know more about dragons than the emperor knows about the black jade blossom, and *that thing* gives the entire province life under his command." She puts her hands on her hips. "Don't bother denying it."

"How?" I whisper.

"Like recognizes like," she says, educating me. She's a dragon too...yet, I've never been able to tell another dragon from their human form. I glance at Song in the corner. "Don't you worry about her. Song knows we're both able to shift.

"And no, there's nothing wrong with you. My gift is the ability to recognize gifts in others. I have relatives from Zhao Wu, but I'm decidedly with Yan Lui and the emperor."

It dons on me. "*That's* why your general kept you so close. He knows your secret."

"Yes, he does. Now, take this. I can already tell those injuries will be painful when you transform."

My thanks is cut off as Liling bursts into the tent.

"What's all this?" she demands, looking around. "And why does she get to wear a kimono while we have to languish in these hideous uniforms?"

"Leave the dragon be, Liling," Daiyu instructs.

"*Must* we tell *everyone*?" I ask indignantly.

"Please. While *you* keep running off with the spies, *we've* been working behind the scenes *here*, Mulan." Liling waves a hand at me. "I know you want to think you're the only special one here, but you're not."

"Actually," Song speaks up. "I'm the only one who *is* normal here. Which, I suppose, actually makes me kind of special."

"You're *very* special, sweet child," Daiyu assures her. The older woman makes a face at me, but I don't understand her meaning as she nods to the small girl. I ignore it, focusing on Liling's comment instead.

"What does she mean?" I glare at Liling. If that girl is a dragon too, I will throw a dancing fan at something.

"Liling is a skilled fighter, Mulan. The girl you met a few days ago was just an act. Liling can kill half the enemy in their sleep if we set her on them."

I raise my eyebrows, looking at her to confirm. She smiles sweetly, drawing a blade from her belt and twirling it in her hands. "Wait until the lieutenant finds out about us, dragon girl."

Clearly Liling joining the army wasn't the accident she claimed it to be. I can't tell if I'm impressed or nervous.

"At least *you* won't be tortured, Liling," Daiyu says. "I have the general's protection if it comes to it, but Mulan has nothing."

She turns to me. "We keep our secrets here, girl. Should anything happen, the four of us stick together. Your brothers can be trusted too since they obviously know about you and are protecting you."

"Brother, singular," I correct. She catches on to the fact that Lan doesn't actually exist.

Daiyu raises an eyebrow. "Well done. You and Liling are good at creating stories around here."

"The point is, if anything happens, we protect each other," Liling concludes. And we keep our mouths shut."

"Let's go!" shouts from outside the tent call.

"Mulan, you'll have to wear the kimono," Song says holding up a needle. "I'll finish this while we fly."

I nod, excited I get to wear a kimono for a little while.

Outside, most of the tents are down and being packed on dragons' backs. I pick my way through the crowd to find Jinhai. Liling runs after me.

"I'm traveling with you," she announces. I look back at her, fully prepared to tell her no but the look on her face stops me.

"The silver dragon predicated your attack earlier while you were gone. That's why the lieutenant sent the team after you. I don't buy it, but I'm also not going to ignore her."

I wait for her to continue.

"She was spouting off about more attacks. You and I need to have each other's back if anything happens and we have to...step in."

"Fine," I respond. Before I can finish, she bolts ahead of me toward Jinhai. When I arrive, she's already secured her passage.

"I'm riding with you." She looks gleefully at me.

Unfortunately, now that I know she's basically a trained assassin, I can't kill her for going after my brother. *Charming.*

Jinhai transforms, putting on a bit of a show for Liling as she stands beside me clasping her hands like a lovestruck child. We climb on and I let the smaller girl sit in front of me.

Twilight sets in as we take to the air. The weyr flies spread out in case of attack to prevent everyone from being hurt at once. The clouds swirl around us and Jinhai propels us forward.

Liling's words swirl in my head. It's possible the silver dragon has the gift of seeing what is to come, but I've never heard of that as an actual gift. Something seems off.

She could have guessed about the attack. She could guess about any upcoming attack and be right—especially since we're at war.

I reconsider when we spot a rebel camp below us preparing to shoot cannons into the skies.

Chapter 13

THE FIRST ROCKET GOES UP, BARELY MISSING ONE OF our dragons. I scream a warning and Liling picks up my cry. Jinhai jerks in the air, nearly tossing us off as he darts away from the enemy camp. Others holding equipment and people do the same, preserving what they can while the rest stay to fight.

Jinhai lands bumpily and tips to dump us from his back. He looks at me and lets out a sharp noise. I know he means for me to stay put.

"Go!" I shout, knowing the others need help.

I rush to help dragons unload what they carry, ripping and pulling as fast as I can. With my knife, I regrettably cut the ropes we'll have to replace later, sending equipment crashing to the ground.

In turn, dragons lift up around me as we free them. A few of the men shift once set free, helping us unpack the others. Once they're mostly clear, I leave the girls and a few men—including Xun—to finish and run through the small line of trees to see the battle. I'm careful not to let Xun see me sneak away before he does.

Chen's rebels have started to shift, leaving their cannons behind to take to the skies. My scales ache inside of me, begging to be released.

Looking over my shoulder, I check to see if I'm being watched. When I discover everyone left is still preoccupied with the last few dragons, I decide to use the opportunity to transform into my dragon state.

Jade scales form and my wings unfurl. I run, leaping into the air to take to the skies and hurdle myself toward the fight. Dragons cry out with war shrieks around me as I join the battle efforts.

Keung wages war against another dragon, his red scales dancing gloriously in the fading light against the sky tinged with navy. A second enemy dragon moves in to help his friend. I don't see Jinhai, but I can help Keung, so I race to his side.

I shriek a warning to Keung, letting him know of my arrival. He calls back as I whip past him toward the second dragon as he launches his assault.

This time, I don't hesitate. Using my fiery breath, I push flames at the orange dragon attempting to collide with me. He reels back in surprise, faltering in his flight.

Dipping in the air, he loses his balance and I charge at him, slamming into him with the side of my body to knock him to the ground. He lands loudly, screaming in pain.

As I turn, Keung is clawing at the green dragon. Neither refuses to bend. Keung yells out, challenging the beast. The green dragon cries back and tries to bite Keung's neck. The lieutenant turns, avoiding the bite, and surprises his attacker by catching his throat in his mouth a moment later and ripping a gaping hole into it. Bleeding, the dragon falls.

I follow protocol and use the movements we were taught in training to work with Keung in battle. Together, we take two more enemy dragons out of the war. Their bodies lay at strange and terrifying angles on the ground below us.

As a line of dragons forms to attack our men, I pull away from Keung and lift higher into the air. I dart as high as I dare, watching the enemy below. I note their movements and translate them into what I learned from the last battle—if their directions hold true through all of their army factions, I know their next move.

Slowly I position myself. The enemy is unwise to make this so easy for me. Creating a group that I can easily attack will be their downfall.

The air rushes by me as Jinhai joins my side. He flies quietly next to me, waiting for me to communicate my plan. I nod to the group and offer the best explanation I can with noises and motions. He clicks, confirming he understands.

Jinhai pauses, preparing himself to be the distraction I need to destroy the rebels. I watch as my brother glides down gracefully to rally the others. I need Chen's dragons distracted and there's no one better than the blue dragon to draw their fire—I hope it doesn't come at the cost of my brother's life.

I wait in the sky for Jinhai to position himself with several other soldiers. Keung watches to the side, tearing into another of Chen's dragons on his own. From here, it's easy to see Keung is going to race into my plan as soon as he's done with the dragon clawing at his hip—I'll have to be cautious of him as he'll need to cross my path to reach the others and I don't want to hurt him accidentally.

My eyes snap shut one time the moment I see Jinhai taunting the enemy—it's time.

Lifting up slightly, I arch myself in the evening sky before plummeting straight down toward them. I pull my wings against my body to avoid resistance as I dive silently toward Chen's army, only releasing them to slow myself when I'm on top of them.

The sound of wings swooping down upon them frightens the first dragons in the line. I beat my wings, pulsing the air before opening my mouth.

Terror. I'm bringing them terror before ending them.

My fire starts to melt their scales. One by one, they drop, unable to withstand the intensity of my blaze. I take my time, moving slowly over the line of dragons, ensuring they're not just knocked down but damaged enough that they can no longer fly.

The dragons fall or fly to the ground, transforming out of their scales to try to save themselves. Several of our men descend and shift, slaying or capturing the survivors.

Our men hold the line in place for me. Keung and the others join in, lending their fire to the cause.

Exhausted, I dart up into the sky, letting the others battle for a moment. Keung follows me.

I shake my head, trying to tell him that I'm alright. He motions for me to land, but I refuse, waiting to go back into battle as soon as I'm strong enough to throw my flames again.

My eyes widen, stretching my scales as I see a group of enemy soldiers in their human forms attempting to run. I make a sharp noise, motioning to the ground. Keung reels back to create momentum before diving toward the ground.

The red dragon burns a line in the grass. The raging fire blocks the men from escaping. Keung lands as I hover in the sky. He stalks toward them, prepared to keep them from attempting to escape—we need captives to tell us information. Our men in human form rush to his aid to capture the enemy.

We've won the battle—only the remnant enemies remain, though they have no hope. They die today or give in to capture. The noise behind me should startle me, but it can only possibly be our men—I've watched as all of the enemy hover below me in their final attempts at survival.

A low growl sounds and I realize how mistaken my assumption was. I turn. The silver dragon, marred with scars, stares me down.

How did she get out of her cage?

She circles slowly. The woman wants me to know who she is before she attacks. Each beat of her wings is intentionally slow.

I consider dropping. If I can surprise her, I might be able to get help as she attacks. I also risk her catching me in my exhausted state and I don't know if I could save myself if she strikes.

She lunges at me, but only enough to startle me. Dragons don't have expressions like humans, but I can swear she's smirking at me.

The silver dragon circles again, this time nipping at my foot. I scratch at her and she pulls back. Neither of us are hurt.

She's playing games—toying with me until she murders me.

Should I strike first?

As I debate my next move, several dragons below me scream up. I feel the force of the air as they make their way to me quickly.

A loud, ferocious roar erupts next to me as the white dragon appears from the night clouds and rushes at the silver dragon—Xun. The silver dragon woman takes off, racing across the sky. Xun comes to a stop next to me, checking to see if I'm okay. When I nod, he goes after the woman, disappearing into the night sky.

Her threat floats through my mind—thankfully my blood is still intact.

I turn, ready to assure the soldiers coming to save me that I'm fine. Jinhai slams to a stop in the air when he sees I'm safe. The others pull up next to him. He directs them to return to the ground and slowly turns with them once I give him the signal again—he knows I need space from the men if I'm going to return to my human form.

Blinking a few times, I dip in the air, letting the current carry me toward the ground. I have to find a place to land and shift where no one will see me.

My weight is heavy on me. My human form is going to regret what my dragon form did this evening. I crave sleep and hope we'll be using the rebel camp as shelter for the night.

Fire burns brightly on the ground creating a barrier

between the soldiers and the field. The trees have all been burned, removing my hiding place.

On the far side of where the trees once were, the silver dragon's cage sits empty among the supplies we dumped before the battle. Some of our men walk toward it to take an assessment of what is left.

My only option is to use the line of fire Keung created as a barrier to hide my transformation behind. Bodies lay on the far side, but no men or dragons walk the field.

I stay calm as I dive toward the far side of the fire wall, trying not to be noticed. If I landed straight down, my wings would draw attention–the last thing I need. Instead, I fly in at an angle, running in with my dragon feet to slow myself.

I transform as soon I touch the ground, pummeling my human body forward so quickly as I run to stop that I fall, rolling on the ground heavily. I bump and collide with rocks and dirt, but eventually slow to a stop.

Quickly, I jump up, making sure no one has seen me.

Everything hurts. Everything burns. I feel like death has claimed me.

"Mulan! Hurry up!" Liling shrieks, waving me over to a small hole in the fire wall that burns high above our heads. She coughs and sputters but waits for me to stumble to her—she must have been watching for me.

I hurry, but my feet are slow. Accidentally dropping to my knees, I pull myself back up, struggling to reach her.

"Pull yourself together," she hisses at me, wrapping her arms around me to support me. "We were checking on survivors and got trapped but we found a way through. Got it?"

I nod, coughing. For a fire breathing dragon shifter, it's a wonder I'm having so much trouble breathing in the smoke.

We emerge from the flames. My kimono rustles around my ankles comfortingly. As I look up, the soldiers all stop and stare.

"They're looking at you, warrior," Liling says. She lets go of me and straightens. "The flames backlighting us must make us glorious—*act like it.*"

She's positioning us in the minds of the soldiers as great and fierce warriors. The embers fly up around us, glistening orange against the now-black sky around us.

Jaws drop and we walk toward the men. Liling's right, this was smart. We'll be given more credit now.

Jinhai runs up to me, grabbing my hands. He pulls me close and turns to Liling.

"I'm okay, lover boy." She smirks and walks past him. The girl is good, I'll give her that. Maybe she can give Jinhai a run for his money—I might not mind her after all.

His body jerks against me at her reaction—I'm going to use his crush against him later.

"Mulan!" Xun calls after he lands and shifts from his white scales in the distance. He rushes toward us.

"Mulan," Keung's nearby voice cuts off my gaze, forcing me to turn away from Xun as he approaches. Liling is by his side, still telling him of my bravery during the battle—she conveniently leaves out the part about my dragon form. "I need a word with you first thing in the morning. I have a mission for you.

"And tell Lan thank you for his help tonight.," he continues, back to the line of men watching us. "I'll need to speak with him soon."

Keung pauses before offering me the most alluring smile I've ever seen. "First thing tomorrow, Mulan."

Jinhai's muscles tighten around me but he doesn't say anything.

"Tomorrow." I nod. No matter how hard I try, I can't get Keung out of my head. I watch him walk away and want desperately to go with him.

"Mulan." Xun breathes a sigh of relief. As he reaches me "Are you okay? You disappeared..."

In the distance, a single lantern goes up—a warning of some kind. I chose to let other soldiers deal with it.

"Everything is okay, Xun," I assure him softly. I quickly tell Jinhai and Xun what happened. They both agree to go after Keung and tell him the silver dragon escaped and tried to attack Lan after they take me to Daiyu, knowing I need someone to check me after the battle.

Sleep now. Find out what my lieutenant wants in the morning.

Chapter 14

"GOOD MORNING, MULAN." KEUNG'S VOICE WAKES me from my sleep.

I sit straight up, clutching at the blanket covering me.

"What are you doing here?" I demand.

"Waking you, obviously." He pulls his face back from me, smiling. "We have a mission and after what everyone says you pulled last night, you're the one I need on my team."

I push his shoulder back, putting more space between us. *So much for keeping our distance.*

"I'm sure she's exactly what you need, Lieutenant." Liling beams behind him, sitting on a crate. "Well, I've got to go cook."

She slides off the box and ducks outside of the tent, leaving us alone.

"What mission is this?" I ask before he can speak.

"Some of the survivors decided they wanted to talk during the night. It sounds like there's a group of Chen's men embedded in the village west of here that might have been working with the men from last night." He smiles. "We're going to see what we can learn."

"Okay," I agree. "You're going to have to let me get dressed though."

"Actually, you're going to need to wear the kimono. We're blending in today."

I watch him for a moment as he looks at me. Keung is sitting on the ground, one knee pulled up against his body with an arm wrapped around it. He's wearing civilian clothing and has his hair tied up.

"This seems like the opposite of not being together," I remark.

Keung leans forward and smarmily grins at me—he's the boy I met at the hospital again. He tips his head to the side before speaking.

"Well, I promise no kissing on this little mission of ours, how about that?"

I purse my lips, trying to suppress the surprised giggle rising up in my throat. I tip my head at him.

"I can behave myself if you can, Miss Lin." He leans forward again. "We have four women in this camp and you're the only one who can convincingly play my wife, and it's far too suspicious if a group of men walks into the village, so it's this or nothing."

"Wife?" I nearly shriek.

How can we go from not seeing each other to married so quickly?

"What do you say? Be my wife for the day, Mulan? I promise I'll be respectable." A sad look crosses his face for just a moment—not even long enough to be sure I'd really seen it. "I'll stay out of your way for you and your new friend. This is just a mission."

"Fine, I'll be your wife," I say dramatically, trying to lighten the mood. I toss the blanket off and spin to face him head-on. "But you're buying me breakfast while we're there. I like Liling's cooking but I'm tired of stew all the time."

"Deal. Let's go." He stands up and starts to leave.

"Hang on, husband. I need a minute to do my hair." My words stop him. "If I'm going to be a proper wife, I'll need to look the part."

"Many women leave their hair down during the day."

"Yes, but we're not living there. If it was a normal workday, I would. Clearly we're just wandering in and a traveling wife wants to make a good impression. I need to do my hair."

"Oh!" Daiyu's shocked voice fills the tent as she steps inside.

"The lieutenant needs me for a mission. Can you help me with my hair?" I ask before she can comment further.

Without saying anything, the medic winds around the boxes in the tent and kneels behind me, deftly working my locks up into a twisted design. Keung watches her hands thoughtfully as he studies what she does. He sits back down, waiting.

I nearly add my hairpin back in, but I don't know where Song packed it for our travels. I thank Daiyu when she's finished.

"Be smart out there, Mulan." She nods, releasing me.

"We will, thank you."

Following Keung out of the tent, we earn stares from the men. They watch as I walk by, the perfect image of a wife. Folding my hands in front of me, I let my long sleeves drape down. I've always loved sleeves like this because they give me something to do with my hands while I'm walking—I don't have to figure out what to do with them like I do when I'm in fitted sleeves.

A team follows us from the campsite to the village, but Keung pulls back, giving us a little space to talk.

"How do you feel about being in charge now that the general is gone, Lieutenant?" I ask, making conversation that hopefully isn't too personal for us now that we're keeping our distance.

"I was prepared for this. He's been planning it for a

long time now." Keung tips his head back slightly so I can hear him easier.

"I didn't realize your father was a general...."

With his hair tied back, the end brushes the top of his shoulder as it dangles from where the rest of it's tied up in a red piece of ribbon. His civilian clothing fits him perfectly as if it were tailored just for him.

"You're right, that didn't come up. I'm sorry. It must have been a shock for you when you found out."

"I was certainly surprised, but it makes sense. You fit it well."

"Do you think?" he turns to look at me out of the corner of his eye. "I'm trying to be a good leader."

I reach forward, placing a hand on his upper leg in front of me.

"I think you're doing very well, Keung. If I didn't know you from before, I'd certainly follow you into battle based on what I've seen of you as a leader. How are you feeling about the responsibility of all this?"

"Honestly?" He pauses. The horse shifts under us as he navigates a dip in the hill. "It's terrifying. Overseeing so many men—and women, too, apparently—is a lot scarier when you're the one with the final say."

"You seem to be managing it well." I withdraw my hand, realizing I've left it on his leg far too long. "I'm proud of the way you've stepped up...even if it *is* your job."

"Thank you, Mulan, that means a lot."

"This really weighs heavily on you, doesn't it?" He nods at my words. "I'm here for you if you need me."

"Boundaries, soldier." His tone is serious, but the smirk he tosses me over his shoulder tells me he's joking. "Good news, wife. We've arrived."

The others wait quietly in the trees as Keung and I make our way into the rows of buildings and head toward the Center where the merchants are likely gathering for the day.

I wrap my arms around his waist as we get closer, our horse moving easily down the streets. Our mount carries a few bags of worthless clothing and some menial supplies—enough to make it look realistic if we're searched but nothing we'll be sad to lose should we have to dump the bags.

Once we reach the Center, we dismount. Keung leads the horse with one hand and offers the other arm to me. I loop my hand around his elbow and gently place my free hand on top of it, anchoring me to Keung's side.

We pass by several merchants, ignoring their wares. Keung makes small talk with a few men as I silently stand by, trying to observe everything around us while he distracts people.

On the ride into the village, I discovered our true mission was to find out where the silver dragon is as well as getting a count for how many of Chen's men are residing in the village. I search for women I can befriend who might be chattier than their male counterparts.

"Here," Keung's voice pulls me out of my search. I look up, smiling at him as a new bride would look at her husband—at least I hope that's what I look like. "I promised you breakfast, did I not?"

I can smell the food from across the street. Keung leads us over to a table full where a merchant is standing, trying to entice us to buy from his offerings.

The warm food sends energy through my hands. Keung watches me until I take a bite, making me feel self-conscious. I nod and bat my eyelashes at him, confirming I enjoy the meal to the merchant.

"She eats so daintily," the man says to Keung. "You've won a prize there."

Suddenly, he grows skeptical. "How come you aren't fighting in the war? A strong young man like you should be fighting for the emperor."

"My brother was sent from my family," Keung replies knowingly. "My bride and I have only just wed this month after the soldiers all left. I'll be called for the next conscription, I'm sure, now that I have a family and home of my own."

The man eyes him, one eye squinted but finally nods. "Well, off with you then, before the emperor calls you in."

"Thank you for the food," Keung replies, paying the man and turning me to go. He picks up an apple and feeds it to the horse, slipping the man an extra coin.

The food warms my entire body. Keung reaches over, pulling a piece of bread from my hand.

"Hey."

"You have to share, wife." He grins. "Don't pout. I bought you breakfast like you asked. I'm a man of my word."

He waits a beat before adding, "I like this."

"Like what?" I take another bite, gaze swinging around at the other merchants' tables.

He leans into me. "*This.*"

Keung pulls another bite of my food and pops it into his mouth. The horse follows obediently over his shoulder with the reins merely draped over Keung's chest, dangling in front of him.

"—covered in marks." I tip my head to the side as I pick up a conversation between two women. "She must have made someone incredibly angry."

"That's my cue," I whisper. I hand my breakfast over to Keung, knowing he'll finish it while I'm gone. He takes it with his far hand, using the one next to me to pull my hand to his lips for a kiss. He nods, giving me permission to wander off.

The women stand behind a table of fans and a table of jeweled hairpieces. I eye them, thankful it's something a young bride might leave her husband's side for.

Both tables are filled with color and if it were any other day, I'd have to shop for real.

"These are beautiful," I comment, running my hands over the fans.

"Your lovely husband must buy you one," the first woman comments. Her long blonde hair cascades down her back as she points out her fans.

"Surely he wouldn't want you to travel without something beautiful in your hair," the second woman comments. "Why, it's so lovely. However do you manage such beautiful hair by yourself?"

"Oh, thank you," I murmur, reaching up to touch my hair. "My husband helps me sometimes."

"Lucky women," the second merchant says. "Perhaps a purple jewel for you to match the accents on your dress? I see your man watching you...we could show him how lovely it would look."

She rounds the table before I can object and spins me to face Keung who is watching us with an amused expression. Plunging the pin into my hair, she gestures to him.

"Pretty girls can always get what they want, young one," she murmurs. "Smile."

Keung laughs as I bat my eyelashes at him. He nods, thrilling the woman with the promise of a sale.

The first woman runs around her table, grabbing a fan. She opens it, displaying it for Keung, and holds it next to me. She moves her hand, making the fan sway.

"Hold, hold," she commands. I take it from her as both women huddle around me.

She reaches around behind her, grabbing a second fan and uses it to show Keung how a woman can flirt with it and continually points to me while nodding at him. Dipping her fan in front of me, she twirls it quickly in a tight circle, then flips it in front of her face and waves it rapidly, revealing and concealing her expression. If she wasn't clearly trying to sell her goods to Keung, I'd think she was trying to snag him for herself.

Keung takes a deep breath, pretending to suppress a grin. He rolls his eyes and looks away, glancing back to give his fake wife permission to buy the merchant's pretty things.

"Oh, I can't," I protest. "I wish I could, but I just can't."

What am I supposed to do with a fan while I'm at war?

"You protest too much," the merchant tells me. "Fans are perfect for enticing your husband to do your bidding."

I chuckle. "The only thing that could entice that man to do what I want is a knife to the throat."

She raises her eyebrows. "Oh? You need a stronger method of persuasion?"

Reaching behind her table, she secretly pulls out a handful of fans. They look no different than the rest of the hand fans on the table. I tip my head to the side.

She motions for me to step between the tables and then beckons her friend over. We form a triangle, blocking outsiders from seeing the fan.

The blonde woman snaps the fan open, twisting it in her hand. She tosses it in the air, catching it as it flips. Spinning it once more, something pops, and suddenly little blades appear on the ends of the fan's ribs. My jaw drops open slightly.

The merchant woman grins and twists the fan around more as she shows off the concealed weapon. She raises a finger to her lips, telling us it's a secret.

"That's brilliant," I whisper. I want one. *I want them all.*

"*Now* you can convince him of *whatever* you like, girl." She beams. "Fun in other ways too. Also good for protection."

She turns to her friend, "She won't end up like that girl."

She pulls the fan away as I reach out to touch it. I

desperately need one of those fans. The woman snaps it shut, retracting the blades.

"What girl?" I ask, knowing they mean the silver dragon woman. *Now I'm getting somewhere.*

"How do you know it wasn't *one of these* fans that *did that* to her?" the other woman protests.

"Excuse me, *what girl?*" I ask as they forget about me in their banter.

"*These* protect," she counters. "No one has the skills to do *all that* with *just this.*"

"*What girl?*" I snap. They both turn to look at me, eyes wide.

"There was a woman who came through in the early hours as we were setting up our goods. She was shredded to pieces as if she had been attacked." The fan merchant informs me. "A good-for-nothing husband I'm sure."

"What did she say?" I ask innocently. I eye the fan to make sure she knows she has me on the line so she gives her information freely.

"She said an animal attacked her in the woods." She shrugs. "You want this?"

"An animal?"

She holds the fan close to her chest, looking me up and down. "Yes. An animal."

"Did she seem like she would be alright?" I pretend to be concerned.

"She moved on quickly enough." The second woman replies. "*She* could have used a hairpin."

I smile at her, reaching up to touch the purple jewel in my hair. Playing on these women's pride is wise.

"Did she say where she had come from—I want to avoid it with my husband if we can."

"No," the first woman replies, moving back around her table with her knife fans. She sets them in front of her, waiting for me. She wiggles her fingers in the direction of the woods. "Over there somewhere.

"You want one?"

"I want three." Her eyes grow wide. A smile bursts across her face as she motions to the ones she pulled out. I tip my head indecisively and she pulls out two more, letting me choose from the designs.

I pick dark, bold colors, knowing if I use them, the darkness will hide the blood better. She nods, wide-eyed as I make my choices. I'm excited to reveal my little secret to Keung when we get out of the village.

"Any idea where the woman is going?" I ask casually as she wraps the fans for me. I sort my coins in my hand.

"No."

The second woman looks over, lips pursed in disdain that I'm buying more from her friend. "She said the next village. She is meeting someone—maybe her husband. She said she's traveling far."

I move over to her table and pick a light pink hairpin up. I'll take it back for Ming after the war is over. The woman smiles, turning to tip her shoulder up to her friend —she made a sale too.

Paying both women, I thank them and turn to discover Keung has moved on. I find him several tables down.

When I join him, I step up behind him, running my hand from his stomach to his chest—I don't mind making things difficult for him. He gasps as I touch him, but turns, embracing me. "Hello, my lovely wife."

I smile, pulling back as he starts to lean forward. "Are you ready to move on, my love?

He nods to the man he was speaking with and turns to guide us away. Looping my arm through his, I tuck my hand into my other sleeve, concealing my purchases.

"Don't talk," Keung whispers "Come with me."

I quietly follow him, watching the moves of everyone around us, hoping Keung's instructions didn't have anything to do with nearby enemy soldiers.

When we reach the edge of the Center, Keung pauses, stopping us. He turns, offering me both hands with fingers woven together.

"On the horse, wife."

I shoot him a questioning look, but he insists I allow him to help me on the horse. I drape my kimono over my legs as I ride to one side, allowing my fake husband to guide me.

The lieutenant takes us down several streets, seemingly away from prying eyes. *I wonder what he's found.*

"I've been told," he finally comments, "that there is an area we should check out over here."

My guard goes up.

As we round the final corner, a stunning pavilion sits near a river. Flowers dot the grass and blossoms blow off of trees, while long, dangling branches create a curtain of privacy.

"It's stunning," I murmur.

Keung reaches up and lifts me off the horse. He ties our mount nearby and leads me to the pavilion where a stone bench waits for us.

"I know I promised there would be no kissing on this trip..."

He pulls me down to sit next to him, watching me closely.

Chapter 15

My eyes grow wide as he leans in.

"I promised I wouldn't kiss you, Mulan, but we have to make it look good in case we're being watched—the village is overrun with rebels. Most of those people aside from the merchants are working for Chen."

I draw in a breath. Keung reaches up and twirls one of the loose strands of my hair between his fingers. "Make it look good."

I narrow my eyes. "You know, there's an easier way to make it convincing."

"What did you buy today, darling wife?" He leans back, not taking my bait, but I refuse to pout.

I tip my head, showing off the hairpins.

"Two?" he asks, surprised.

"I'm taking one back for my sister, should we survive this." I reach up, touching the jewels.

"How kind of you." He smiles warmly at me. "And?"

Pulling the package out from my sleeve, I reveal my fans.

Keung's eyes narrow as he purses his lips. "Three? You bought three *fans*? What use do you have for fans?"

"Beauty, of course. Didn't you see how she was flirting with you?" I giggle, leaning into him in case anyone is observing our interactions.

My hand drags over the muscles in his arms and I ache for him to lean forward and kiss me. He can tell—his eyes light up and he leans toward me to taunt me for a moment before leaning back. This has to be as hard on him as it is on me, but he's withstanding my advances awfully well.

"You wasted my money on fans, dearest?"

I pick up a fan, twirling it in my hands. He watches my fingers move along it, spinning it for his approval. Snapping it shut, I raise it to my face and pop it open again, mimicking the women who sold it to me.

Keung watches my every move as I flirt with the fan, quickly at first, then slowly, never taking my eyes off of him.

"See, dear?" I croon, drawing out my words lavishly. "I move it like this, spinning it just so.

"And then...I click this button and the blades pop up,

ready to slice your handsome little face open," I finish sweetly, taking him by surprise. "And that, my loving husband, is why I bought three. I thought it would spice things up a bit."

The shocked grin on his face is almost more than I can bear. "If that's how you spice things up, dear, count me in."

He leans in and I close the fan, setting it on my lap. "Just...not today. Because I promised to behave, and I'll do it even if it kills me."

I run a hand down his chest making his breath catch in his throat. He pulls me toward him making our legs touch and his arms are wrapped around me so I have nowhere else to go. Keung runs his hand up my arm, making me shudder.

"Even if it kills me," he repeats. "But know this, Mulan..."

Keung leans in so that his lips nearly flutter against mine. He buries his hand in the hair pinned up at the base of my neck. I sigh, closing my eyes.

"When this is all over," he growls in a low whisper, eyes burning into mine as I look up at him, "*I am coming for you.*"

My heart slams into my chest, pounding wildly. I shouldn't be indulging this—there will always be wars for him to fight.

"And I *will not stop* until you are *mine*."

My mouth goes dry and heat creeps into every inch of my body. In the months I've known him, I've always known Keung to be a passionate man, but I've never heard him more serious than this moment.

"I promised you once, and I promise you again: when it's safe, you and I will be together."

"Keung," I murmur. I should stop this.

He reaches up and puts a finger on my lips. "We're behaving, Mulan. You should stop talking now."

He smirks and stands, holding a hand out to me. Unable to move, I just stare.

"Come now, wife, we have more of the village to see before we move on." He hides his face from prying eyes behind my hair as he pulls me up and leans in to whisper, "And you still haven't told me what those women told you."

I realize I still haven't told him and quickly turn. "The silver dragon came through this morning while they were setting up. They claim she's moved on and said she had a ways to travel."

Keung nods. "We have no way of finding her, but we need to finish scouting the village and report back. We need to find out how she escaped—someone let her go."

I breathe in deeply, horrified that someone got past us to let her free. Keung reaches up and puts his hand on the far side of my face, tipping me so that my cheek rests against his lowered forehead. He breathes in too, then lifts my hand to kiss it sensually.

I wrap my arms around him, drawing him to me. If he wants to tempt me, I'll tempt him back. I sigh, smiling evilly when he looks down at me.

"Cruel, wife."

"So are you, husband, not giving me what I want."

"You know I can't," he whispers sadly. "Not now."

He turns me, walking us toward the horse. I wait as he unties him. Keung turns back to me, a question on his lips.

"I...I saw you with *him*, Mulan." He looks away, running his hand through the front part of his hair that he left down. "You're not...with him, are you?"

I'm not sure how to answer that. I don't want to hurt either of them, but I'm unsure where I stand with either. "We grew up together, Keung..."

"I won't ask you to wait for me, Mulan. I know that's unfair, but...just...think about what you want. If it's him, I'll step aside, but if it's me...please don't...just...please."

In truth, I'm not sure what I want. I wanted Keung desperately, but Xun feels so familiar. Both obviously care about me, and I care for them, but the entire situation is so confusing that I'd rather battle the enemy than have to decide right here on the spot.

"I'm not trying to hurt you..." I murmur.

"I know," he whispers urgently. "I'm not accusing you of anything. I don't want you to feel pushed, I just want to know where I stand. If I have to watch you with someone else, Mulan, I need to know so I can prepare myself for that."

"I—" My words are cut off by a powerful force. A woman's scream breaks us apart. We both instinctively reach for our weapons.

"I know you!" She transforms before us, trading her human form for vicious gray scales.

The dragon roars, stepping menacingly toward us.

"I take it she was in one of our battles," Keung quips, stepping forward to defend us.

The dragon slams a foot into the ground, shaking it under our feet. Keung tosses a look back at me.

"New plan!" he shouts. "Get on the horse, wife! I'm going to have to shift for this one. Be ready if I come for you."

He sheaths his sword and transforms into his powerful red dragon form. I wish desperately to be able to shift, but even if I did and could play off Lan just showing up, Keung would still be looking for me as Mulan during the fight to ensure my safety—I can't use my dragon form this time.

The gray dragon lumbers toward him, shrieking. I mount the horse, prepared to run at her with sword drawn to plunge it into her heart.

She rears up, spitting fire toward Keung. He retaliates, nearly setting her ablaze—*my* fire would have melted her.

The two engage, battling fiercely. The gray dragon takes to the skies and Keung quickly follows. They dive around each other, clawing and biting. I watch helplessly from horseback, unable to offer assistance.

Suddenly, the gray dragon whips around, diving straight toward the ground in a suicidal plunge. Keung chases after her, closing the gap between them. When she pulls to the side, Keung has to veer to avoid hitting the ground. She uses the opportunity to fly straight toward me faster than I can get the horse to move.

I snap my eyes shut, preparing for impact.

This is how I die.

I hear a loud and terrifying sound—the sound of a scale-on-scale collision in the air. The wind races by me, knocking me off the horse. My hands slam into the ground and I roll, tucking in my head to avoid injury.

When I stand, a white dragon is mauling and mutilating the gray dragon. Xun rips her apart, covering himself in her blood as he viciously defends me.

Keung lands a short distance away and shifts, running toward me. His injuries, thankfully, didn't translate over too badly to his human form.

"It's Xun!" I shout, letting him know we're safe.

At the sound of his name, Xun turns, leaving the dragon carcass in the street. He flies quickly toward me and snatches me around the waist with his foot, lifting me into the air. I scream in surprise, but he doesn't stop.

Turning his head back, he shrieks at Keung and then continues on our path toward our campsite. I wrench around to look behind me, watching Keung climb onto the horse and race after us.

I call to Xun but he either can't hear me or chooses to ignore me. The wind whips against me, somehow feeling much stronger than when I'm riding on a dragon's back.

Xun flies over the trees, taking us back to the camp. I finally give in and stop struggling to see, trusting him not to fly low enough for me to hit something—he's incredibly brave to be so bold about flying out in the open with enemy soldiers nearby.

We land outside of the camp. A crowd of people watches as he touches down, holding me in the air so I don't get hurt. Once he stops, he releases me, setting me upright.

My hands instantly go to my kimono to straighten it. By the time I'm done, Xun has shifted and steps toward me in his human form.

"You're safe," he says, enveloping me in his arms. Xun holds me tightly. "Are you hurt?"

"I'm fine," I respond, shrugging out of his embrace.

"You never should have been allowed to go with him," he mutters, shaking his head. "You should *never* have been put in that kind of danger."

"Were you following us?" I ask as he grows more agitated. I wave off Ning and Wei as they start to approach. They hold back, watching from a distance.

"I was scouting when I saw you. It's a good thing I was there or you could have been killed."

"Technically, I could be killed anywhere...this *is* a war," I correct him playfully. He doesn't banter back.

"This is a ridiculous war," he mutters. "We shouldn't even be in this war. If these leaders would just recognize their place, this wouldn't happen. But no, it's a lost cause and we have to fight anyway."

"Of course we need to fight, Xun. Chen's men took our source of life. Without the black jade blossom, Yan Liu will wither and die." I take a step toward him, trying to calm him as he paces in a tight line in front of me.

He shrugs off my touch, still pacing and talking with his hands. "All this pointless danger. We should let Chen have it and give him control of the province—he'd rule far better than the emperor, and everyone could live."

"And be subject to his rule?" Shock overtakes me. "He's merciless, Xun. He kills all who oppose him. He *started* this war."

"But he takes care of those who side with him, Mulan. None of them suffer as we do here."

"They die the same as we do."

"They live in glory and riches," Xun protests. "His men are far safer."

I look at him horrified. He notices and calms himself down, stepping toward me. I wave Ning and Wei off again as they try to step in.

"I'm sorry, Mulan. I don't mean to frighten you—I just got so scared when I saw that dragon try to kill you. She would have sliced right through you and there was nothing you could do to protect yourself because you're enslaved to an army who would rather torture and kill you than let you transform and fight."

He pauses, taking my hand. "At least the other army reveres their women. They treat them like glorious warrioresses. You should be treated like that, Mulan."

"Not at the expense of killing an entire province to keep something stolen."

Xun looks desperate. He breathes heavily. "Come with me, Mulan. Let me take you away from here. I could keep you safe."

"We can't abandon the army, Xun." My head explodes with questions on his sudden change. *Why is he doing this?*

"You're worth so much more than they're giving you credit for, Mulan. Come away with me—we can be free from this."

"Xun, we can't leave..."

"Come with me, Mulan." His desperation increases as he tugs on my hands. I stay firmly where I am. "Let me make you a queen, Mulan."

"What are you talking about?" Nervousness creeps from the pit of my stomach through my body and out to my limbs. This is wrong. Suddenly I'm glad for Ning and Wei's presence. My eyes dart to them and they slowly inch forward, trying not to draw Xun's attention.

"*Mulan...*" He holds tightly to my hands, not letting me step back. Behind me, noise starts to build. We're being attacked.

"We have to go help," I protest. I fight to step back. From the corner of my eye, I see Wei draw his sword, still walking slowly toward us.

"Let me go, Xun."

"I can't do that, Mulan." He refuses to relinquish my hands, holding me in place. His eyes shift, narrowing. His desperation turns to something else...something harder.

I try not to gasp. The noise strengthens behind me as the battle heats. He refuses to let me run to help the army.

My mind shuffles through the reasons he might be

acting this way—only one makes sense. But it can't be, can it?

"Xun...are you...are you working with Chen's army?" It's unfathomable, but I ask anyway.

"Come with me, Mulan." His words are harsh. "Let me spare you this. When you're my bride, you can help me stop all this."

"You have no power over this," I challenge, twisting to get away from him as Wei and Ning draw closer.

They move, distracting him. I pull away and run.

"Don't do this, Xun," I beg.

"Come with me. We belong together. We've always been as one."

"I'm not like you, Xun." I shake my head defiantly, suddenly realizing the gravity of what is happening. Xun has betrayed us—he was never really with us. "I would never do this."

"You're exactly like me," he shouts. "And you belong at my side. I'll show you—*we're the same*. Come with me and I'll prove it to you. You'll decide to join us once you've seen it from our side! Please, come with me!"

He moves toward me.

"You can't stay here with these people—they'll destroy you! You're not safe here—especially when they find out. You know you're at risk here!"

I move away from him as the men close in.

"Fine," he yells in a harsh tone. "I'll be back for you, Mulan. I promise you will be safe."

Xun shifts, his white scales blindingly bright in the harsh sunlight. He lifts off and races to the battle just as Wei and Ning reach him, avoiding their blades.

They look at me questioningly.

"He's with Chen! Go!" I scream.

They sheathe their swords and shift, racing after him. Closer to the camp, men watch me, preventing me from joining them in my dragon form. Xun was right—at least Chen's army allows women to fly. Still, I would never side with Chen's men as they destroy people to keep what they stole in the first place and condemn an entire nation to death.

I run toward the camp, knowing the men are still watching me—I can't escape and return in dragon form. Behind me, I hear hooves beating against the ground. Keung arrives and races into battle.

If I can hurry, maybe I can catch Xun and talk some sense into him. He hasn't done anything to hurt us yet—there's still time to save him. If he truly cares for me, he'll listen the way he did when we were children talking about our hopes and dreams.

Our men are in the skies, leaving only a handful on the ground with the women as they try to protect our supplies. My eyes dart back and forth, searching for Xun against the brightly lit sky. His white scales make it easy to hide alongside the clouds.

It isn't until I see his sleek dragon form bursting across the sky, rushing right toward Jinhai that I realize what he's doing.

Chapter 16

I scream louder than I ever have before. Xun's promise of showing me echoes in my head.

He races at Jinhai, knocking other dragons out of the way. Xun collides with my brother, forcing him down. He roars, looking to ensure he has my attention.

Rearing his head back, he moves to strike my twin, threatening to take a bite out of his neck. I scream again.

"Xun! Don't do this!" My calls never reach him though. I can beg all I want but he's not going to hear my plea that far up in the sky.

Jinhai grapples with him, but Xun planned his attack carefully, clamping down on my brother so that he can't twist to defend himself. No one else comes to his rescue from the sky, all interlocked in battles of their own.

Keung shifts but is immediately attacked, pinning him to a battle on the ground. No one can save Jinhai but me.

I can keep my secret and watch my brother be severely hurt or I can shift in front of Keung and face the army's wrath as a woman with wings.

Two more dragons join Xun in attacking my brother. My battle cry startles them as I shift, but it only ignites Xun—he's won.

He quickly releases Jinhai so one of his friends can take over. Xun sinks to the ground to watch as I fly murderously toward the dragons hurting my twin.

Jinhai has managed to turn, facing his attackers. Able to defend himself again, I decide to take out the closest dragon, letting him fight the other. I slam into him, pushing him away from my twin.

Once he's far enough away, I abruptly stop, putting just enough distance between his traveling body and mine to melt his scales off. I scald him mercilessly as he drops out of the sky, screaming in agony. I wish I could feel bad.

Turning, I catch Jinhai's attention and he plummets, giving me the opportunity to burn the second dragon. I follow him as he falls, ensuring both are dead by the time they hit the ground.

Whipping around, I search for Xun. He stands in his human form, waiting for me.

I drop, shifting before my feet touch the ground and I hit heavily, bouncing from the force. I use it to launch myself at the man who betrayed me.

"If you think revealing my secret is going to get me to come with you, you're insane!" I growl, rushing at him.

"You're not safe here—you know you're not." He crosses his arms defiantly. "I was never going to hurt your brother, for the record."

"Those marks in his side tell a different story." I point behind me, motioning to the bloody marks on my brother as he flies somewhere in the distance. "How could you betray us like this?"

"I've never betrayed you, Mulan. This is *always* who I was."

He was a spy when we met as children?

"How could you?" I demand an answer.

"I only want to protect you, Mulan. You're the only one who's ever understood me—"

"How could I understand you? I didn't even *know* you." I keep my distance. Fire ripples in the grass beside us as the fight continues overhead.

"I came here for you, Mulan, to make sure you were protected. Just let me protect you."

"You're *putting* me in danger!" I protest, flailing my arms out to the sides as if it emphasizes my words.

"I killed *my own* soldier for you *minutes* ago, Mulan," he screams angrily. "I killed the man in that house to *protect you!* I stopped the others from even *entering* it and finding you where they could hurt you. I ended those spies in the woods so they couldn't hurt our plans and start a battle before it was time to keep *you* safe!"

He killed our spies.

"You weren't supposed to be a part of this. You were supposed to be in your village safe from the war so I could find you and take you out of there when this was all over." He shakes his head. "When I found out you were here, I rushed to you. I've done everything to keep you safe!"

"You told Chen's army where we were and when to strike. How?" I demand. "How did you communicate with them?"

And how did he find out I was with the army?

"I protected you, Mulan. They all had orders to keep you safe."

"Yet you had to kill your own soldiers to stop them from hurting me. Sounds like you have quite the bit of control here, Xun."

Xun looks up into the sky behind me. Jinhai screeches as he approaches, letting me know he's coming to help.

Scrunching up his face, Xun makes a decision.

"I told you I wouldn't hurt him," Xun calls, preparing to shift. "But I will be back for you, Mulan. You are my queen and I promise I won't let this war hurt you. You'll sit at my side when all of this is done."

Xun shifts, darting into the sky.

"No!" I scream as Jinhai tries to fly after him. He

hears me and stops, landing beside me and shifting.

Xun races away, taking the enemy dragons with him, ending the battle. Our men chase them for a moment but at Keung's roar, they drop back to the earth and wait.

Jinhai turns to me, terror on his face. His pulse beats wildly in his wrists as they bump against my shoulders as he grabs me.

"We have to get you out of here," he yelps, wild-eyed.

"Keung saw me." I can't outrun this.

It's up to Keung what happens next.

"You've been a good soldier." I try to protect my twin. "Deny knowing about my ability to shift if you have to or tell them I forced you to pose as Lan."

"We're in this together. If we go down for this, we burn together."

He turns, wrapping his arms around me as we both face Keung as he makes his way over to us quickly. We stand together, waiting to face our punishment for our deception.

Keung looks livid.

I hurry to tell Jinhai everything I know about Xun in case we can use it to our benefit.

"You're a dragon?" Keung seethes as he steps within hearing range. He stops several feet away, glowering over us. No one is close enough to hear us yet.

"Don't hurt her. We're on your side," Jinhai begs. "We

didn't tell you because that woman attacked us and we didn't want Mulan to suffer the same fate because people didn't take the time to listen. She's no threat to you."

"She lied." Keung's betrayal radiates across his face and body, tightening every muscle.

"She lied to keep me safe," Jinhai replies, tightening his grip on me. He moves us back and Keung steps forward. "Lieutenant, please!"

"Xun is working with Chen." I can't tell what's going to happen, but Keung needs to know this information before he locks me up and banishes me. "I don't know how he found out I was with you, but he came here to take me back with him."

I suddenly realize how badly that sounds for me, but I can't stop.

"There must have been a spy here that sent him that information, though I don't know who. But Xun killed our spies in the woods, and he killed our men when we went on that mission for you. He's been working with Chen the whole time and I didn't see it. I'm so sorry, Keung."

He reels back as I say his name.

I whisper, "You know I wouldn't betray you, Keung." I fight back tears.

"Xun deceived us, why wouldn't you?"

A tear trickles out, dripping down my cheek painfully slow.

"Please, Keung. *You know me.*" I try to appeal to him. "I'm that girl from the hospital you talked to every day— the one that you teased mercilessly and started to have feelings for. I'm the one who took you to safety and sat beside you every day until you were well again. *You know me.*"

His face cracks and he swallows visibly, trying to sort his emotions and what he knows is right tactically.

If I were in his position, I wouldn't be able to trust me either. I can only hope for his kindness.

"You saw her, Lieutenant," Jinhai calls to him. "She never hurt any of our men. She fought with the army and saved us several times. She's always sided with you. You can trust her. We're with Yan Liu and our actions have proven that!"

"You made up a fake brother..."

"Yes, we did," Jinhai admits. "I thought you might hurt her and I made it up to protect my sister, and then we had to see it through."

"So that was *you* out in the woods?" Keung pieces our lies together.

"Yes, *I* spoke to you, but *she* is the jade dragon."

Keung sighs, examining us as the men get closer.

From what I can tell, no one else noticed me shifting. If I can get Keung to keep our secret, we might be able to move forward.

"We know you might not be able to trust us—" I start.

"I do," Keung cuts me off. He adds quietly, "I trust you."

I gasp, jerking back into Jinhai—we've been spared.

"Tang Xun betrayed us! He's working for the enemy." He turns to address the other lieutenants and remaining general as they reach us. "We will hunt him down and cut him off."

"Prepare the camp—we're leaving this evening. While you're preparing, I'm going to find us answers. Move out!"

Keung motions for us to follow.

We rush behind him toward the tent as the other men return to their human forms behind us. He points for Jinhai to go in and work with the other leaders. Grabbing my hand, the lieutenant pulls me away.

"Not a word of this to them," Keung hisses at my brother. "Go tell them about Xun while I handle this."

"Wait, where are you going?" Jinhai calls, worry in his voice as he watches his superior pull me away.

"She and I need to talk. You go work with them on a plan. We'll be back after our mission." He pauses. "She'll be safe. I won't hurt her."

Jinhai mumbles behind us but I wave him off as Keung drags me across the field. His hand is tight around my wrist and I have to run to keep up with his driven strides.

Chapter 17

Keung leads me deep into the woods as the sunlight starts to disappear, moving so quickly I can't keep up. He holds me up as I stumble behind him.

My heart is beating wildly as he turns, slamming me into a tree. His arms go around me, circling me tightly. His lips are harsh against mine, forcing my eyes shut and prompting me to raise my hands to tangle them in his hair.

I whimper as he moves our lips together, grateful he believes me.

"You lied to me." His words are harsh and low, holding his grief.

"I'm so sorry," I whisper back, begging him to forgive me. I turn, unable to look at him. "I'm so, so sorry."

Tears stream down my cheeks as he kisses me roughly again—it's as if he's trying to communicate without words.

My hands run over his shoulders and arms, pulling him toward me. "I didn't ever want to hurt you, Keung, I was just..."

"Protecting yourself and your brother," he finishes for me, pulling back. "I don't ever want you to have to lie to me, Mulan. I want us to trust each other like we did before."

"So do I," I murmur against his neck. He groans as my lips float over his skin. I bury my head against him.

"Then I have to tell you something," Keung whispers, pulling back from me. His hands grip my upper arms tightly. He's as much of a wreck as I am.

I nod, waiting.

"You have the gift of intensity to your flames," he starts. "We don't all have such strong gifts, but I do."

I wait, watching him. Keung takes a deep breath.

"I wasn't honest with you either."

My organs drop inside my body. Coldness runs through my veins.

"Mulan, when I was in that hospital, I kept something from you."

My grip tightens around his forearms. I'm not ready for whatever this admission is.

"Mulan." He pauses. "I could have healed myself."

I tip my head involuntarily to the side, confused. "What do you mean?"

"You found me unconscious in the field that day. You took me to the hospital and when I woke up, you were there. I could have healed myself, but you were taking such good care of me. You were sweet, and you took all my teasing so well."

He pauses, looking at me from under his bangs, hair still tied back from the mission. "I wanted to see more of you, so I stayed."

"You stayed in a hospital for two months just so you could spend time with me?" This was not the admission I had expected. He smiles a little and nods.

"I knew I wanted to be with you more and if I was healed, I'd have been sent back to the fight."

"You suffered through all that for two months...for me?"

He smiles bigger. "When you know, *you know*, wife."

I laugh—I can't help it. His smile radiates across the space between us. He looks relieved, the stressed look melting away.

"Forgive me?" he asks.

"If you can forgive me for being the jade dragon." I smile back at him and he moves closer, wrapping me in his arms again. I feel secure pressed between his body and the tree—Xun can never find me here. I feel foolish for ever kissing that man in the first place.

"Now that I know, I think you can be a real asset to us,

Mulan. We just have to keep the others from knowing—I don't know how they'll react given the only women dragons out there are working for Chen."

"I understand. I need to tell you about Chen's army, by the way."

He nods. "I'll try to block for you when I can so you can shift more often. Please just be careful up there."

No restraints. No restriction—a girl could get used to this.

"Come with me," he whispers.

Keung takes my hand and we walk to a cliff. Sitting just inside the tree line on a fallen trunk, we watch the sunset together. The skies dances in brilliant pink and purple colors.

Gently, he leans into me. "We'll talk in a minute."

His lips are tender as he guides our rhythm. I pull on his bottom lip slowly, tracing my hand over his arm and cradling his neck. He smiles under my touch.

I arch up under him, tilting my head back to open our kiss more. Sighing, I move so I can wrap both arms around his neck. He pulls me in closer, lifting me until I'm in his lap.

"So much for not kissing on this mission," he mutters.

"Just couldn't stay away, could you?" I tease. My tongue grazes over his as I lean in.

"Not with you trying so hard to make me fail." He breaths sharply as I bite my lip.

We go back to kissing, enjoying our temporary freedom as the sky shifts beside us. The colors flail behind my eyelids as I get wrapped up in Keung's embrace.

When we can't breathe, I finally pull back, breaking the trance. Keung's lips are swollen and his chest puffs in and out as he watches me.

"So, are you going to tell me what that was about back there?" His smile fades. "He was yelling pretty emphatically at you."

"Xun is a member of Chen's army," I inform him sadly. "I had no idea. Apparently, he *was* even when we were children—it must have been a ruse to scout the province before the war started."

"I'm sure they were planning it for a long time. You can't just steal something like the black jade blossom without knowing what you're doing. We had that thing guarded so well and they still managed to infiltrate our ranks and take it. I still haven't figured out how they did it —saw that thing every day and I thought it was *impossible* to access."

"You *saw* it?" I ask, tilting back a bit. "How did you have access to the black jade blossom, Keung?"

He moves his eyebrows up slightly. "Yeah, I guess that's the other thing I have to tell you."

Keung pauses dramatically, waiting for me to ask. I don't, refusing to give him what he wants.

"I grew up in the emperor's palace."

I'm impressed. I start to ask more questions, but he continues.

"Not just as a general's son." He smiles. "The general, Mulan, *isn't a general.*"

He waits for me to work it out. It takes me a moment, but I get it.

"So *that's* why he could do whatever he wanted without checking with anyone—he doesn't answer to the emperor because he *is* the emperor."

"Yes, he is."

"Which makes you..." My eyes grow big. He holds me as I lean back.

"Yes. And now you know why I was so worried about us being together and being caught...because they wouldn't be holding you against a lieutenant general, they'd be holding you against the future of the entire kingdom."

I breathe out slowly. I've been kissing the province's next emperor.

"Xun knows about us," Keung continues. "I don't know if he's worked out who I am yet, but if he has, it's even more dangerous for you."

I sigh. "He wants me as his queen."

"He *what*?" Keung's voice drops.

"Before he left, he tried to convince me to join him with Chen's army. That's when everything went sideways."

"He's in love with you." He says it as a fact, not a question.

"So he says. We hardly saw each other as kids, but apparently I stuck with him."

Keung untangles himself from me and stands. He offers a hand and pulls me up.

"He's not coming for me because of *you*, Keung. He wants me because he wants *me*. Staying away from you wouldn't have done anything to change that, so can we please let this ridiculous notion go?"

"I *hated* seeing you with him," he admits.

I reach up and tuck his hair behind his ear. "Got a little jealous there, did you?"

Keung tries to suppress a smile. "Maybe."

He leans down to kiss me softly. When we pull away, we stare at each other for a moment before turning to return to the camp—so much for scouting.

"Tell me about the black jade blossom," I prompt.

"The emper—um, my *father*—uses it to purify and enrich our waters, among other things, which you already know. It's kept in a vaulted room inside the palace in the center of a large crystal pool. The waters flow from the pool to streams and springs outside the palace and then continues on to the fields and crops.

"With it, everything is strong and preserved from the weather, elements, and intentional corruption. Without it..."

"Without it, everything is weakened and everyone suffers. We're subject to the mercies of climate and our enemies. Chen is trying to cripple us."

"Yes." He nods. "My father is the only one who is allowed to activate it—it's the emperor's job. It takes a piece of him each time, which is why only the emperor is allowed to touch it. It's a sacrifice for the people—to give life to all, someone must sacrifice."

Keung raises his hand, lifting a branch up for me. I duck under it, waiting for him to follow.

"What does it take from him?"

"A bit of his power. You saw at the mountain how he was able to conceal us—that's his gift. Each time he reenergizes the black jade blossom, he weakens. He's able to build it back up over time, but never to his full strength, which is why he can't do it for the army all of the time."

"When we retrieve it, and you take over for your father, will this be your job?" I ask, suddenly concerned for him.

"Yes, it will be my responsibility and *honor*."

I want to argue with him, but I can't contradict the reverence in his voice. This is his duty and he's prepared to take it on proudly, no matter the cost to him. I'm proud of Keung.

"Besides," he adds, seeing my hesitation. "My ability to heal myself is vastly different than my father's. I'll be alright."

We talk until we reach the camp. Joining the others, we prepare to take flight. I remain assigned to my brother for transportation.

Morning sparkles along the river as we wake. We stopped in the early morning darkness to set up camp. The light reflects off the water, blinding me as I open my eyes from under my blanket—we didn't bother setting up the tents.

I sit up, watching the scene for a moment with arms wrapped around my knees. It's easier to bend in my uniform than my kimono. If only we weren't here waiting for another attack, this would be a stunning sight.

"Shame we have to leave," Song says quietly behind me. I twist to look at her. She scoots over close enough that our arms brush against each other.

"How are you doing with all this, Song?" I ask as she rests her head on my shoulder.

"I think I'm the only one who ended up here accidentally," she jokes sadly. "I wish I wasn't."

"I wish you weren't either." I sigh. "We'll keep you safe though. Daiyu has been practicing with you, right?"

I've been so busy, I haven't even been able to check on the small girl.

"I'll be fine. The lieutenant has men keeping an eye on me and the supplies during the fights." She pauses. "Umm, Mulan?"

I turn, looking at her. She stares at the water. I squint as I try to see what she's looking at.

"Something's not right," she whispers. Her voice grows louder. "Mulan, something isn't right."

Whipping around, I stare down the water, trying to figure out what she means. All I can see is the glittering sparks of light bouncing off the water rippling in the breeze.

"What is it, Song?" I murmur.

"There." She points. "There are men in the water. They're here."

"How do you know that, Song?"

"I...I'm not sure." There's no way Song should be able to determine something I can't—she's not a dragon which means she can't have a gift like that. Unless somewhere in her background there's a hint of dragon's blood—which could explain how she knew I was coming back to the tent that time.

If the water is able to conceal men, there's only one thing that can do that—the black jade blossom. It must be nearby.

"You're sure?" I ask. She nods, her entire body starting to shake in fear.

"The river!" I scream, standing. "We're under attack!"

Around me, the entire army rises to their feet, swords and arrows ready.

"What's happening?" Daiyu's voice sounds behind me but her words drop off as Chen's men rise up out of the river at our sign of aggression.

Water drips off the men, rolling off their bodies as if they hadn't been under the water at all. The black jade blossom's power over water isn't typically used this way —at least not in Yan Liu—but I've heard stories about what it's capable of doing should the emperor want to engage its powers that way from my father's time serving.

Our army raises their bows and launches arrows at the men standing in the water. A wall rises up in front of them, swallowing the arrows and plunging them back down at their feet. Chen's men respond by launching their own arrows at us the minute the wall of water drops.

We scatter, pulling back to avoid them. A dozen of our men fall, arrows protruding from their chests.

Our men shift, transforming into their dragon states but Chen's men hardly seem to notice. They shift too, donning their scales, and turn to make their way toward their mission—me.

Chapter 18

"No!" Jinhai yells, realizing what's happening. He rushes toward me. "Protect Mulan! They've come for her!"

Keung echoes his command somewhere in the distance and the remaining men pick up the chant before shifting. I push Song away, trying to keep her safe from the oncoming dragon assault.

"Get her out of here," I command, forcing Daiyu into action to protect the girl.

My twin crashes into me. "Get back." He pushes me behind him.

In front of me, he shifts, knocking me backward with his tail. The others attack the oncoming weyr viciously, engaging in a bloody battle. Wei rushes to defend me alongside my brother. From above, Ning hovers over us, waiting to make his move.

I try to see around the dragons protecting me, searching for Xun, but the white dragon is nowhere to be found. Cries fill the fields as dragons rip and tear into each other mercilessly. With my bow and arrows in hand, I take aim, attempting to shoot around my brother and friend—my arrows do nothing against the dragon scales.

"There you are," a man hisses behind me. He reaches around me, pinning my arms to my side. "The general has been dying to get his hands on you."

He tugs me backward and I scream, biting down on his upper arm—the only thing I can reach. He bellows in my ear but refuses to relinquish his grip on me. Slamming my heel into his shin, I force him to double over, giving me enough leverage to throw myself back and slam into his face. He curses as Ning descends on us and quickly shifts to his dragon form to protect himself.

The black dragon clutches me with his foot, lifting me into the air and tramples backward to avoid Ning's waiting claws. Pulling a dagger from my belt, I wait to strike.

A brown dragon collides with Ning suddenly, knocking him away from us. The enemy rips into his side, tearing a chunk of dragon flesh and dropping it on the ground. Ning roars in pain.

Jinhai and Wei are viciously attacking a group of four dragons trying to make it past them to me but jerk their heads away and call to their friend when they hear his suffering.

I dig my blade into the black dragon's foot. He drops me and I make it a few strides away before he claws his way back to me, slicing at my flesh as he lifts me higher into the air.

My weyr pushes toward me, battling Chen's army to keep me safe without knowing why I'm the object of the attack. I'm sure some of them guess it's because of Xun's betrayal, but I know it's more than that—Xun knows my secret and has seen my flame.

Jinhai turns, leaving himself exposed to the dragon he was fighting and rushes toward the black dragon. Behind him, the navy dragon claws, leaving unsightly gashes down my brother's back and side. Jinhai holds in his screams and digs his claws into the ground to propel himself forward to me. I shake my head violently for him to stop and protect himself, but he won't.

Throwing his head back, he summons his flame and directs it toward my captor's haunches. It distracts the black dragon enough that Jinhai is able to attack. One of our men reaches us, clawing at the black dragon's other side.

After several agonizing minutes, the black dragon drops me and I fall to the ground, bumping against his scaly body along the way. I drop my blade as I strike the ground and scramble to pick it back up.

I run toward Ning, hoping I can help. Keung, in his red dragon form, flies toward us from the other side of the fight, dodging dragons in the sky. He crashes into the dragon attacking Ning and slams him into the ground, knocking him out. Keung deftly puts an end to him and then lands, preparing to defend me.

If only Ming were here—her gift of amplification might allow Keung to use his healing gift to save Ning and the others. Ning transforms, dropping into his human form on the ground.

"Ning!" I grab at him as I reach him, examining his injuries. In human form, they aren't nearly as bad, but he needs medical attention immediately.

Daiyu rushes to my side. "What do you need?"

"Where is Song?"

"Liling's got her. I couldn't stay; there's too much to do out here."

Daiyu pushes me aside, working on Ning as he groans. "You should make yourself scarce, Mulan. They're not going to stop."

"I'm not leaving."

"Your precious little boyfriend has come for you. You know what will happen if they get you." She glares at me, reminding me how Chen's army will use the jade dragon.

I suddenly remember that the black jade blossom must be nearby—I need to tell Keung. "You've got this?"

She nods as I dart away. Tears fill my eyes as I hear Jinhai cry out, but I can't stop yet.

"Keung, it's me!" I scream a warning as I leap onto his scaled back without him seeing my approach. I crawl out onto his neck so he can hear me. "They couldn't have altered the river without the black jade blossom—it must be nearby! You need to find it!"

A dragon slams into him, knocking me from his neck. I scramble back on the ground to avoid being hit.

I have to find the black jade blossom.

Before I can get very far, I'm pulled into the air. The dragon's grasp knocks the wind out of me. His approach was concealed by the other sounds of war.

He lifts me high into the air. Calling to the other drag-ons, they look up at him. Upon seeing me in his clutches, far from the rest of my weyr, they turn, leaving their battles and take to the skies to protect him as he absconds with me in his grasp.

Keung looks up, crying for me. Jinhai tries to fly only to be knocked back down by his injuries. Wei and several others take off after us, but the teal dragon holding me has the advantage of a head start and an entire weyr blocking for him.

More of our men rise into the air, following quickly

behind us, but they won't make it in time. I only have one choice.

I pause, checking the ground bellow me as we fly over injured and dying dragons on the ground. We make it over the river before I pull my blade and driving it deeply into the teal dragon's leg. Unlike last time, I drag it as far down as possible before the blade hits my own body, leaving a gash long enough to pour blood from. It rains down on the dragons below us.

He drops me and I plummet toward the earth.

Wind rushes around me. The feeling of weightlessness is terrifying without my wings to support me. My hair flies around me, making it hard to see. I try to keep my scream in.

I shift, transforming into my jade scales in front of everyone—there will be no escaping this if I survive.

Thrusting my wings out, I catch myself, slowing my descent. Before I hit the ground, I have my ability to fly back and lift myself into the sky.

Anger fills my vision and I narrow my darkened eyes until they're slits that I can barely see out of. I hone in on the teal dragon above me and use the rage building up inside to launch myself at him.

Seeing me, he rushes toward me—either out of stupidity or because Xun didn't tell him about my flames —and attempts to burn me into submission. My flame reaches him first and he reels back as if I threw embers in his eyes. It only infuriates him.

Clawing at him, I prepare to throw my flames again, this time catching his underside. He falters, dipping enough for one of my weyr to take him on as he sneaks up from beneath us.

I turn in the sky, prepared to fight back the dragons now turning to face my oncoming army. I feel my gift grow, shifting and changing—perhaps a byproduct of the black jade blossom being nearby or perhaps from my rage or fear as I see Jinhai and Ning on the ground in the distance.

The scent of melting dragon scales is an acrid mix of molten metal and decaying corpse. The wind thankfully carries it away from me as I take out an entire line of Chen's dragons. Their bodies fall from the sky and crash into the field and river.

Enough bodies block the river that the water over-flows, gushing onto the land. I swoop low enough to finish incinerating the ones blocking the water, knowing it could cripple the villages who rely on it in the distance. Ashes tinge the water, but it doesn't fight back—the black jade blossom must be further away now.

As I return, the weyr is locked into a relentless siege in the air. I cry out, warning my men to get back. Many of them untangle themselves, flying out of the way for me to unleash my blaze at their enemy counterparts.

Wei sidles up next to me, prepared to fight alongside me. Together with his burnt orange scales and my jade, we must look like a giant pumpkin in the sky, but only Liling and Song—and the injured soldiers—would know from their place on the ground watching the entire weyr battle above them.

Screaming fills the skies, but I drown them out, focusing only on Wei's movements next to me and the dragons I have to fight. Keung races up to me, gesturing wildly.

It takes a moment, but I finally understand his plan. He darts away and I wait for his signal. On his command, Wei, Keung and I scream at the top of our lungs. Our lieutenant dives down, instructing the others to follow.

I'm left alone in the sky with two dozen dragons.

My heart beats inside my chest. I use the sound of my wings flapping to control my heartbeat. Chen's army turns on me, seeing their opportunity to capture the one they're after. They seem fearless as they take off in my direction, unafraid of my deadly flames.

I wait. They need to be closer.

A number of the dragons pull off, rushing away—they must have the black jade blossom and are trying to protect it.

I wait. *Not yet.*

From the corner of my eye, I see a flash of white—Xun. He waits for the dragons that abandoned their team and leaves quickly with them, not daring to come for me himself.

I wait. *A little closer.*

A dragon's gift always comes at a cost. The general can hide others but at the cost of his health. Keung can heal himself but at a cost to himself as well. My fire burns inside of me, scorching my insides as I hold it at bay, waiting for the precise moment I need to release it to destroy Xun's men. Pain radiates through my being, but still, I wait.

When they're close enough to attack, I open my mouth. Creating a wall of fire in front of me, I shield myself. The dragons don't stop. The first to reach me perish instantly, melting and disintegrating before my eyes through the harsh flames.

I inhale, readying the next blast. They don't stop.

Xun must have given them the directive of not returning without me. They refuse to back down.

I melt them.

Bodies fall, crashing into the ground. Everything rattles under us.

The dragons on the outside of the attack still feel my flames, scales falling off their bodies with the intensity of my heat. Blood trickles down, dousing the men below.

Leaving my position, I jerk up in the air, flying over the remnant. Like a waterfall, I spew my fire over their backs. They arch and careen out of the way. Some manage to dodge me, finally choosing to flee and face Xun and Chen's wrath.

I chase them just enough to ensure they will leave and not return. Turning back, I find what's left of the army watching me from the ground in their human forms.

Slowly, I fly to them.

I land and shift.

It feels nothing like walking out of the fire that night when they all stared in awe. Now it's a mix of fear, accusations, betrayal, and gratefulness.

I run to Jinhai's side, throwing myself on the ground where he lays. Someone managed to pull him next to Ning, making it easy for me to check on both injured men. Wei stands next to them, wobbling on his feet. He clings to one arm, obviously injured.

Liling and Song run up next to me and I rattle off a list of medical supplies I need to help the boys. Song takes off, scrambling to get it quickly—I'm sure my hysterical voice prompts at least part of her swiftness. Liling lowers her stance by my side.

Murmurs rise up around us as everyone circles in.

"You'll be okay." I run my hand through Jinhai's hair to move it out of his face, brushing Ning's arm with the other.

"Move!" Keung's voice commands somewhere behind the line of soldiers.

Wary eyes watch us, but I keep my head down, focusing on stopping the bleeding. Both will live, but it won't be easy for a while.

"Is she one of them?" I catch the comment in the crowd.

"What about her brother?" another asks.

"She burned them—she *has* to be working with us."

"So did Tang Xun and you see where that got us!"

Arguments blossom around us but I can't listen. Liling shifts positions, ready to defend me if need be.

Keung bursts through the crowd and Liling eyes him carefully. He turns to address the men, standing between me and them. Song reappears, bringing me my supplies.

Turning, I catch sight of the man who's tongue Keung cut the tip off of on our first day. He glares at me triumphantly.

I work with my back to Keung as I bandage my brother and friend. Wei kneels down to help me.

"Way to keep a secret," Wei hisses. He offers a smile to me to soften it. "We could have helped, you know."

"It's always been a secret," Jinhai replies, gasping as I push on his wound. "Don't let them hurt her."

"I'll protect her," Wei promises. "I think Keung's got it, though."

I tune back into Keung as he addresses the men.

"Oh, *I've* got her," Liling murmurs, fingers balling up at her side. I have no doubt she's got a couple of blades on her ready for use should anything happen.

Song hovers next to Ning, helping me bandage the boys. I hand her material to wrap his chest with and she tries to lift him up. Reaching out, I take his hand and pull to help her.

Keung raises his voice to address the concerns being shouted at him. "Mulan and Jinhai have proven their loyalty to Yan Liu and to me as their commanding officer. Despite their deception, we will allow them to continue serving with us, this time with Mulan as a dragon fighter. If you have an issue with this, you will come see me, but you will not hold them under suspicion from this point forward."

The remaining general and lieutenants nod at his words. I'm sure Daiyu's general is on our side given the secret he's hiding as well.

"Chen knows how powerful Mulan is—his army will be back for her. We need her fire to win this war—we will protect her at all costs, am I clear?"

The men agree.

"But sir—she lied to us. She deceived us!" a man shouts.

"And she will be reprimanded for that!" he cuts them off. Keung turns. "Come with me."

I try to protest but his sharp demand forces me to my feet as Daiyu appears and takes my place. Liling takes a step forward as if she's going to come with me. "Watch them. Don't let them near him" I motion to Jinhai and Wei, worried someone will approach my brother for being a part of the deception. She nods, settling in to protect Jinhai.

I rush behind Keung—he said I would pay for what I did. He's going to have to do something to appease the angry crowd.

We step into the sole tent we set up last night after arriving. The fabric door closes behind us.

Chapter 19

"THEY HAD THE BLACK JADE BLOSSOM," I SAY AS SOON as we're alone. "You heard me say that, didn't you?"

Keung faces away from me. "Yes, I heard you."

I had expected him to drop the hard façade when we stepped out of view of the others. Instead, I'm greeted icily. This punishment might be worse than I thought.

"Xun was there in the distance," I try to continue.

"I'm sure he had it with him. The water would have had much greater force had it been closer to us—I've seen what it can do. It's how we won the last war with your father." Keung clasps his hands behind his back. With his feet shoulder-width apart and his back straight, he looks fearsome paired with his curt replies. "We'll retrieve it. The emperor feels it's call when it's activated like that— I'm sure he'll be joining us soon. He left us to track it, and if it was here, he's likely nearby."

I'm quiet, waiting for him to say more. When he doesn't, I take a step forward.

"Keung," I whisper, stretching out a hand toward his back. "How bad is this?"

"You transformed in front of the entire army—an army who fears women dragons as the enemy. Did you really think that was going to end well, Mulan?" He tips his face slightly but doesn't look at me over his shoulder.

"I had to escape. I was falling—I didn't have a choice. And then I had to save...them." My explanation sounds pathetic.

Keung turns slowly, features much softer than I expect.

"I know. I saw." He grins. "Did you really think I was going to lecture you?"

He played me.

"Well, I thought I could get out of it...through...*ways.*" I shrug. "But I guess if that's not needed..."

I start to slide away, turning around, but he grabs me and pulls me close.

"You were magnificent. And now your secret is out so you don't have to hide anymore." He leans in, waiting for me to kiss him. I give in.

When he pulls back, he adds, "I'm reprimanding you *very strongly* right now, for the record."

"Is *that* what we're calling this now?" I joke. "Because

I think if that's the case, your reprimand isn't strong enough."

I put a finger to his lips as he leans in. "Oops, missed your chance."

Keung chuckles as I pull away from him.

"What *is* my actual punishment for this?"

"Demotion."

"You can demote a first-time soldier who isn't actually an intentional part of this army?" I say in a monotone voice. He shrugs.

"Lieutenant General!" a voice calls from outside the tent. "You need to see this, sir."

"Look upset," Keung whispers. He forces his face into a displeased look, furrowing his brows and tightening his jaw before opening the tent for us to step outside. I attempt to adopt the same look Ming gets when she's scolded for something at home and follow him outside.

"What is this?" I breathe.

In the distance, lanterns float in the sky. Red dots against the blue sky float quietly upward. I can barely make out the other colors so far away.

"It's a distraction," Keung murmurs, squinting to see. "Chen's men know we're here. They know we defeated them in battle and nearly got the black jade blossom back. I'm sure it's a message to their people, but also a way to try to lure us out. The only question is, are they really there and trying to get us to overthink and look elsewhere or are they really trying to draw us to that spot because it's an ambush?"

It's a lot to consider. I try thinking about what Xun would do, but I never really knew him in the first place. If it were me, I'd send it from my location and assume they'd overthink it.

"What if it's not a distraction at all? What if they're calling us into battle?" I suggest. "We're weakened. If they have reinforcements there, they could crush us. And even if they think we'll look elsewhere first, *someone* will have to check the lantern location. At some point, we *have* to end up there."

The lanterns float gracefully in the distance. Before the war started, once a year, the entire village would gather for a celebration that ended in magical lanterns floating in the sky after dark. Each was graced with tassels and an intricate design on the paper.

I waited each year for that evening and made a wish on the first lantern into the sky, my own lantern, and the last I could see as they floated away. When lanterns from another village passed by, I whispered my wish and closed my eyes.

I close my eyes now and wish we could find a way to end Chen's tyranny. When I open them, Keung is watching me.

"What do you think we should do? Should we engage them?"

"Why ask me?"

"They came for you, Mulan. Xun must hold some kind of power in Chen's army. You know him better than any of us, therefore you should have some input in this." He pauses as I stare at him. "A good lieutenant knows how to use his resources."

My commanding officer turns, stepping back into the tent.

"What are you thinking?" He takes a seat at the table motions for me to join him. I slide into the chair next to him.

I stare at the maps rest on the table for a long time. I can feel my frown deepen, pulling down the skin around my eyes. Moving my lower jaw, I try to work some of the tension out.

"I have an idea!" I shout suddenly, jumping out of my chair. Keung starts next to me, gasping at my sudden movement.

"Okay, what is—?"

"I'll be right back." I sprint from the tent, leaving him sitting there in surprise.

Heads turn as I rush by, but no one says anything. They watch me quietly as I search the crowd. It takes a few minutes, but I find Daiyu kneeling by an injured man a few feet from Liling and Song as they stand over the boys where I left them.

Pulling them aside, I quickly explain my plan.

"I want in," Song says.

"No," Daiyu and Liling say together. I'd prefer she stay behind too, but it's her choice. We might be more believable with her at our side.

The young girl raises her eyebrows defiantly.

"Whatever you four are talking about, I don't like it," Jinhai calls over. I glare at the girls to keep their mouths shut.

"Focus on recovering," I call back. Tugging on the girls' arms, I move them away. "We have to speak to the lieutenant."

Jinhai tries to sit up, but Wei holds him down on our behalf.

"He'll be fine, by the way. I gave him some of that concoction I gave you. It should help."

"And Ning?" I inquire.

"He'll also be fine," Song replies. I get the feeling she might be developing a crush on the older boy. I wonder if I could get Wei to go for Daiyu, even though she's a handful of years older than him.

When did I turn into their matchmaker for real?

We walk through the army together toward the tent,

making our way to where our leader is waiting. Keung looks surprised to see us all.

"I've found our secret weapon," I announce.

"Oh?" Keung looks curiously at me. "I thought you and your fire were our secret weapon."

Daiyu smiles. "She's not the only one, Lieutenant."

Keung's grin fades. "You *all*?

"No, just Daiyu," Liling replies. "I'm just a trained ninja."

She pulls out a set of knives and twirls it in her hand. His jaw drops, making Liling smile deviantly.

"And what about you?" He looks to Song.

"I just want to help." She looks to me to further explain. "After all, there are no female dragons in Yan Liu."

"That's right, none at all, except for me." I smile, waiting to see if he catches on. "When Chen's men come across us, left behind while the soldiers are out scouting, they'll assume we're easy targets."

"And if they recognize you?" Keung cuts me off, leaning back in his chair.

"They'll still never suspect Daiyu can shift, and they certainly won't see Liling coming. And Song can hold her own as well."

"When they take us to their camp, you can follow— we'll lead you right to them," Daiyu adds. "They won't suspect a thing when we attack from within their camp and you boys can follow as back up."

"And since we're inside the camp, we'll be able to scout first. We can determine if the black jade blossom is there and where their leaders are hiding within the camp so when you enter, we can tell you exactly where to focus your attack."

"And if they recognize you and torture you, Mulan?" He's searching for flaws, looking to make the plan better.

"Xun won't let that happen."

"So, you're saying you're about to walk willing into his clutches?" He shakes his head. "I don't like this."

"You won't be far away, but yes. We want you to let them capture us, give us a day to scout, and then follow with an attack. It's the only way we can learn how they're operating."

"We've kept our secret this long, Lieutenant. We can do this," Daiyu adds. She pushes her long brown hair over her shoulder and waits for an answer.

"What if they keep you where we can't see you for a signal?" Keung asks.

"We'll have a predetermined time of attack. Twenty-four hours after time of capture," I inform him. "You'll only come in early if we signal you. We'll work out every detail, Keung. I promise it will work."

The girls whip around to look at me as I use our

commanding officer's first name. Keung's eyes grow wide. I shrug, pretending I don't know what's happening.

"*Mulan?*" Liling demands an answer. I shrug again, wide-eyed. I haven't told them about us and I don't plan to.

Keung stands up from his seat. Slowly, he walks toward us. Wrapping his arm around my waist, he pulls me back so that he can sit against the table and hold me. He glances over at the girls.

"Oh. I'm sorry. I thought we were doing the transparency thing." He grins and shrugs, pulling me closer to nuzzle against my chin and neck. "Just between us, of course."

Their jaws drop. I can practically see the glow of my red cheeks reflecting off Keung. I stay quiet.

Turning, I try to wriggle away from him, but Keung grabs my hips and pulls me back so I'm sitting high on his leg as he rests against the table. He wraps his arms around me and holds me, resting his chin on my shoulder.

Song looks thrilled. The other two hold their reactions closer.

"So, are we telling the rest of them you can shift?" Keung asks.

"*Are we telling the rest of them you've claimed the jade dragon and that's why she's not getting in trouble for lying?*" Liling challenges.

"If he punishes Mulan, he punishes us *all* for keeping secrets, Liling. Shut up," Daiyu explains. "I don't think there's any way to avoid telling them—why else would we be sending three defenseless women and your most important dragon into the enemy's hands?"

"True. So, let's talk details." Keung motions for everyone to sit, finally releasing me from his grasp. We take a seat and discuss strategy until General Yu walks in on us.

The general took the news surprisingly well. As Keung expected, he had felt the black jade blossom's presence and confirmed it had been here.

I left Keung to explain the rest to him. Wandering into the woods, I gather herbs we need for our wounded soldiers. Daiyu and I spread out, hoping to cover more ground.

My bag is nearly full when something catches my eye. The movement startles me. Straightening, I watch closely, searching through the trees.

"Surely you can see this is madness, can't you, Mulan?" Xun's voice floats around a tree.

"Why are you here, Xun?" My hand drops to my blade.

"Come with me, I beg you." He steps out from behind the tree trunk and holds up his hands to show me they're empty.

"You attacked my brother." I take a step back.

"To get you to take action," he counters.

"You sent your men after me," I protest taking another step back.

"To bring you to my side, my queen." Xun steps toward me, dropping his hands. His stride is longer than mine, diminishing the distance between us by half.

"Do you have the black jade blossom, Xun?" I ask, knowing I need to get as much information as possible.

"I'm not going to hurt you, Mulan, you can leave your blade where it is."

"I highly doubt that given what you did to Jinhai."

"I'm sorry he was hurt, my love." He takes another step. "You should bring him with us. We'll welcome you both with open arms."

"You don't have the power to do that, Xun. It's not your army."

"They listen to me." He frowns. A branch snaps somewhere, calling his attention away for a moment. I can only hope it's Daiyu and she can run for help—we're not that far from camp but they can't see us hidden in the trees.

"Do you have the black jade blossom, Xun?" I force his attention back to me.

"No, the king does. He allowed us to use it to try to reach you through the river though."

"Where is Chen, Xun? Are you with him?"

"I can take you to the king." He reaches out.

"He's not with you?" I need more information.

Another snap from the woods. Xun turns. "I have my own army to run, Mulan. Come with me and I'll show you."

If I want more information from Xun, I have to play along. Stupidly, I step toward him.

"You know I can't," I say, pretending to be sad.

"You can, Mulan. You can come with me now. I'll take you to Chen and we'll welcome you. I hold power with the army—we could run our own province when this is all over." Xun steps closer, taking my hands in his. "We have the black jade blossom—once this is over, we'll have everything.

"Please, Mulan, everything I've done since the first time we met was to build this for you. I kept coming back *for you*. This is all for you."

I look around, hoping it looks like I'm nervous we'll be caught. If he actually thinks I'd consider leaving with him, he might believe my act.

"What is your plan, Xun?" I whisper. "What is the end game here?"

"When Chen controls Yan Liu, we'll turn Zhao Wu

into the richest, most feared kingdom. His army will continue to defeat the provinces around us and his rule will provide for us all." Xun looks like he actually believes the delusion.

"How do you know he'll keep his word to you, Xun? What if he's just using you?"

His face drops, guard suddenly up. "You're not coming with me, are you?"

Xun's grip tightens on my hands. I try to stay calm.

"I just need to know what's happening, Xun. I'm nervous without details." I stammer. I have to make him believe me—it's not working.

"No, you're trying to gather intelligence. I've known you long enough that I can tell when you're being sincere or when you're trying to be a good little soldier." He tugs at me, trying to force me along. "Come on. We're leaving."

"Let go." I struggle. Xun pulls on me harder, pinning me against his side. "Xun, let go."

"No. You will work with us whether you like it or not, Mulan. Chen has need of your fire. You either come with me now, or I'll force your compliance."

"Are you going to try to kill my brother again?" I spit, fighting against him as he threatens to do something to force my obedience.

"No, Mulan. You have this delusional idea that Jinhai will survive against me. I don't want you getting any ideas in that pretty head of yours to try to trick us." He glares at me. "Capturing your brother won't do me any good—I'll bring you Ming instead. We'll be waiting for you with the others where you saw the lanterns."

"You wouldn't."

"It will only take me a few days to go back and get her, Mulan. Don't think I won't."

"She's a *child*." I pull away from him. He lunges at me, catching my arm just enough to knock me off balance. I topple forward, dragging him down with me.

Xun pulls at my feet, trying to force me back to him as I attempt to leave the trees. I kick, but his weight holds me down.

"I'll leave your sister be if you stop fighting against me, Mulan." His hand digs into my hip. "One day you'll see this is for the best."

"You're delusional if you think I'm ever going to choose to be with you."

I turn, slamming the heel of my hand into Xun's face. He releases me just enough so that I can shift. Adopting my jade scales, I tower over him, but Xun is quick and follows my lead.

I screech, warning the others of his presence and he growls dangerously at me. Xun nips at me and I prepare to throw my fire at him.

He circles me, lashing out with his teeth. I attempt to

burn his tail but he doesn't flinch. After a moment, he lunges at me, starting a brawl.

Slamming his body into me, he flips us over. We roll, smacking into trees as we claw and bite at each other. His teeth are sharp against my side but he avoids anything fatal. In turn, I go for his neck but can't quite bring myself to do permanent damage—my heart screams I can still save my old friend even though I know I can't.

The noise we're creating must draw the army to us, but I'm too caught up in the fight to notice if anyone has come. My injuries bleed, as do Xun's, but we don't stop.

A loud roar sounds next to us, breaking our concentration. We both turn to see a mighty dragon standing next to us—it rushes for Xun.

I crawl out from under him, struggling to stand.

He calls to me one more time as he scrambles away from me. The plum dragon rushes forward. Xun knows with his injuries, he can't fight the dragon. He struggles to fly but manages to lift into the air and race away.

The plum dragon immediately shifts and runs toward me—Daiyu. I drop into my human form, collapsing on the ground.

Chapter 20

"Can you get up?" Daiyu scrambles to my side.

I run my hands over my body to see what injuries translated over. It feels like I bruised a rib, but I feel mostly okay. "I think."

Standing, I hold my hand against my side and let Daiyu support me.

"He'll need medical attention," I blurt. "He said he wasn't with Chen, so if we can beat him there, we might be able to get into the camp without him knowing.

"Daiyu, he threatened my sister." Fear creeps from my chest out through my arms to my fingertips. I don't think Xun would stand a chance against both of my parents, but if he brought his army with him...

"How?" She pushes us forward, out of the trees. A line of our men stand ready, weapons in hands. "He's gone!"

"He said he would find her and use her against me."

"Fine, if he goes back to the village to get her, then this is our chance. Xun could destroy our plan but if he goes for her, we can get in and rescue her when he arrives."

"I don't like—"

"You don't have a choice. We have to move. Now." She motions for the men to get out of our way as we rush by.

I straighten, standing on my own. We break into a run.

"Xun said he'd bring her to where the lanterns were— that must be where Chen and the black jade blossom are."

"Then that's where we go."

The cart bumps roughly over the terrain. Song huddles in the corner of the cage, playing into the illusion—though I doubt she's faking it. Daiyu sulks, looking angry while Liling fidgets.

"Let us go!" I slam my hand against the wooden bars. They weren't smart enough to bind us—they assume we can't shift.

"Shut up." The man scowls, turning around to glance at me. "You're lucky you're alive at all."

In the process of getting ourselves captured, two of

our men died at the hands of Chen's rebels—they sacrificed themselves for the cause. Daiyu's general almost didn't let her come, but Keung talked him into it.

It took an entire day for the enemy to notice our small faction sitting by the end of the river an hour from their camp. I'm nervous Xun made his way back.

My eyes drag over every hill, cliff, and ledge we pass. I try to memorize the land, but it all blends together.

I move to the back of the cage and sit by Song, wrapping my arms around her to lend her my bravery. She taps my arm twice, assuring me she's okay.

The men pull us into the camp and we're suddenly all alert. We sit up, watching the men and women stare at us as we're dragged in. Several of the men nod, grinning viciously. The women all raise their eyebrows and look away—we're not dragons so we're not good enough for them.

Music trickles over to us from somewhere in the center of the encampment. It starts slow, transitioning into a faster traditional song from Zhao Wu. It reminds me of my mother. She taught me to play when I was little. It twangs gently.

The men stop the cart near a group of tents. The man who had been pulling us walks away, commanding the others to watch over us. Slowly, soldiers start forming a circle around us to gawk.

"Look at those pretty dresses," one comments, stepping closer.

We shift to the center of the cage, keeping as far from the open bars as possible. We have to endure this to get to Chen.

Another eyes us, waiting for a nod from our guard before approaching. He runs he hand up one of the bars. "Won't the king love you. Perhaps he'll share when he's done with you ladies."

If I had my blades with me, I'd slice a finger off for him. Chen's men took our weapons when they captured us, as we knew they would.

"What's all this?" Our captor walks back after a few moments. "Back to work!"

He saunters over to us. "King Chen will see them when he's finished."

The wait takes forever. I study the crowd, looking for faces I might recognize, but I don't see anyone that I remember being connected with Xun's team. Maybe we outran him...or maybe he was here and left.

Carts of food sit nearby. Everything looks lush. The black jade blossom has clearly served them well. The man sees me eyeing the fruit and walks over, picking one up and taking a dramatic bite out of it. He smiles, crushing on it so that pieces dribble out of his mouth. It's disgusting.

Peeking around the corner of a tent far enough away that I have to squint is a stack of lanterns. They're as colorful as I imagined when I saw them in the sky from our own camp.

The music shifts, its pace picking up. My fingers move along my leg as if I were playing. I bury them in my kimono skirt so the men can't see.

"Well, this is something," Daiyu murmurs.

"No talking!" the guard next to us slams his elbow into the bars, rattling them. Daiyu goes silent, bowing her head to fit the role of a meek woman of Yan Liu.

We sit in silence for another hour, listening to the men talk about us from a distance. Finally, a man walks over for us.

We're pulled from the cart, each escorted by a man on either side, gripping our arms tightly. They force us forward, through a line of tents until we reach a massive tent that's triple the size of the meeting tent for our army —it's like they stitched several together.

Outside, poles hold up an awning over the entrance. Inside, the tent is divided into sections. Loose fabric rustles between the rooms they've created, weighted down to keep it somewhat in place.

The men push us forward as we protest, digging our heels in the way they expect us to. The light coming through the fabric tinges everything with a yellow glow.

Bits of dust float in the air, catching and sparkling in the light.

A woman stands in a section off the main tent, half hidden by the loose fabric. She folds something with her back to us. In another room, a concubine sits draped in loose, flowing fabric as she waits. She lifts her eyes as she hears us walk by.

A group of men fills another space, speaking quietly in some sort of meeting. We're pushed by them quickly.

When we reach the back of the tent, a man waits for us. His hair is brown, cut off at the chin with a single section that would flow down his back were it not tied up for battle.

His arms are covered in metal, black laces running around his forearms. This must be Chen—he seems to tower in front of us, but he can't be any taller than the rest of the men in either army.

He turns slowly, clasping his hands behind his back. His eyes gleam as he looks us over, but he acts unimpressed.

"Welcome to the new Zhao Wu, ladies. Your presence is most welcome."

My heart stops. Fear races through every inch of my being as he steps near. *I recognize him.*

My hand nearly floats to my hair and I'm grateful to have woven it up so intricately. Make up covers my face, making me look different than usual. He hasn't seen me in years—he might not recognize me.

Chen steps forward to inspect us.

"I've known Yan Liu women to be quite agreeable, so I hope that is the case for you, ladies." He looks Liling over slowly. "I understand you came here as captives, but I hope you will leave this conversation as my honored guests."

He reaches up, fingering a strand of Liling's hair. She swallows, refusing to make eye contact—she'd probably kill him on the spot if she did.

"But first, I need to know where you came from. Perhaps you could enlighten me?" He hovers in front of Liling.

"We were taken from our camp an hour from here," Daiyu answers. Chen turns to look at her.

Skipping over Song, he steps in front of Daiyu. "And why were you with the emperor's army?"

"Our villages were attacked, sir. The army took us to protect us."

Daiyu suddenly drops to her knees in front of Chen. Behind her, the guard pulls back his foot from where he kicked her.

"You will not be so informal with the king," he declares. "Bow!"

I nod to the girls and we all slowly crumple to our

knees, tucking our chins in, but we refuse to stretch out with hands before us as is expected in the presence of an emperor.

"Stand," Chen commands. When I rise, I find a satisfied smirk on his face. Stepping back, he continues to examine us.

"What else do you know?" He crosses an arm over his chest, raising the other to his chin.

Chen's gaze fastens onto me.

"Nothing, your highness."

He brightens. "Ah, a maiden who knows how to show respect. I like that. Perhaps we could get to know each other better."

"I prefer not, your highness."

The usurper looks like I slapped him.

"You would prefer to *work* for me then? Those are your options, after all: work for me or serve as a concubine. Shall I put you to work or offer you as a reward for my men?"

"We'd like jobs, your highness," Liling offers, drawing the attention away from me.

He still hasn't figured out who I am, but I know exactly who he is. Chen narrows his eyes at Liling. In her blue kimono, she looks stunning—we should have dressed her in bland colors.

Chen is a unique name for him—certainly not the one I knew him as. It fits better for his family.

"What job would you like, little one?" Chen moves from me to stand in front of her again, tilting her chin up. "Can you wash for us? Fetch our drinks?"

"I can cook," Liling offers.

"And have you poison us? Oh, I think not." He chuckles.

"I can sew, your highness." Song's voice is soft as she speaks. "I can teach them, and we can mend your uniforms and make you splendid garments for after the battle."

He appraises her. "Very well. You shall be tested to see how you do. I expect the rest of you to be as compliant."

Chen moves back to me slowly. "*You*, I think, will be kept close. I have a feeling you'll make an excellent decoy to lure your army, and in the meantime, you can stay by my side to assist with whatever I need you to do."

Like father, like son, I suppose.

I hold perfectly still to avoid cringing at the thought of being near Chen.

"We'll work on you." Chen eyes Daiyu. "Remember, ladies, that if you slip up or if we catch you out of line even once, you will join the ranks of our concubines. You're very lucky I've given you this opportunity at all, but I have a final battle to plan and don't have time to train you right now."

He motions to the guards who step forward and lift us off the floor. "Take them to Lanying."

We're dragged backward out of Chen's personal area. He watches as we go. Just as I'm pulled out of the makeshift door, Chen turns, moving to a box tucked away in the corner. Xun's father opens it carefully and it glows—the black jade blossom.

Wheeling us into another of the pretend rooms in the giant tent, we're pushed in front of a woman. Her black hair sparks with a tint of blue that's accentuated by her elegant red kimono.

I catch sight of the markings first on her hand as she spins to face us, then up her chest, out onto her neck and shoulders and up into her jawline—the silver dragon.

Chapter 21

"What have you brought me?" She croons, studying the other girls. She gasps when her eyes fall on me. Moving closer, she squints and the scales etched into the skin by her eyes to mark her as an enemy crinkle.

"That is all." She waves off the guards. They wait outside her fabric door.

Moving closer, she reaches for me, lifting my chin up. She's lucky I don't bite her.

"He didn't recognize you, then?" The woman tips my head to the side. "Clever girl with the hair and makeup. You won't be so quick to fool your lover though, now will you?"

"What do you know of this, silver dragon?" I growl, alerting the others in case they hadn't recognized her.

"I'm known as Lanying here, little pet. And I know a *great many* things." She lifts her hand away from me, grasping them together under here long kimono sleeves in front of her stomach. "I know you're not here by accident."

"Your master's men caught us," I challenge.

"If they caught you, you wouldn't be here looking like a concubine." She wrinkles her nose at me.

"I'm acutely aware Xun is looking for me."

"Yes," she smiles. "He is. But that doesn't explain *this*. You aren't here to wed him as he'd want. Why all this?'

"His army knows me. I hoped to avoid this if I weren't recognized."

"Hoped to avoid them knowing you're the jade dragon that's been terrorizing our men in battle?" Her smile grows as I pale. "Yes, little pet, I know about that too."

"Xun told you while he was here..." I mutter.

"Oh, little pet, he hasn't been *here* since he ran off to join your army to rescue you to bring you back as his queen."

Suddenly all of Xun's queen talk makes sense. His father is the king, which would make him next in line.

"Then how do you—?"

"Little pet, you have your fire, and I have my gift."

Her gift *isn't* sight. Her predictions weren't from her gift—they weren't predictions at all.

She turns, picking up a small bottle. The silver dragon sprays herself with something and continues to adorn herself with jewelry. "Such a shame about you, really. You could have made a lovely queen, little pet. I told him as much, but I knew you were too feisty to settle into his plan.

"He just couldn't let his little love go, though, and I can't bear to take that away from him." She turns back around, her smile revealing her pointed teeth. "He wants you for a wife, so you shall be his wife—or concubine *if we must* until he can break you."

"Lanying, why did you summon—" a male voice breaks into the conversation.

She smiles over our shoulders.

"Hello, my prince," she greets him. "I have a gift for you, my son. Your little pet is here."

Xun walks around us, catching sight of me. His eyes light up.

"Mulan." He turns to Lanying. "*How?*"

"Your father's foolish army didn't recognize her and brought her here. I'm sure it's a trap as they were found only an hour from here with only two guards."

"Your father didn't recognize her," she relays.

"He hasn't seen her since we were children." Xun sounds breathy as he speaks, still not taking his eyes off me.

"We should warn him of her deceptions."

"Your father tried to make me his concubine," I

inform Xun loudly, breaking whatever trance he seems to be under.

"He will not touch you," Xun says flatly. "You are mine and mine alone—he promised me as much. Where is the rest of the army?"

"I have no idea. I was brought here by your filthy rebels."

"Mulan, I can make this very difficult for you and your friends," Xun warns.

Xun's head snaps toward Lanying, pausing for a long moment. "Fine," he says as if answering her, though she said nothing.

He looks at her and raises an eyebrow. She tilts her head and smiles back at him as if she's proven a point. Xun narrows his eyes in response.

"You can hear her...can't you?" I murmur.

That's how he knew where to find me. Lanying *and* Xun have the gift of communication. It's how he knew to come back for me today and it's how he knew I was with Keung's army.

"Yes, he told me where you were so we could attack, little pet. Try not to get overwhelmed." She turns to Xun. "Take her to your father. And *bind her* before she shifts on you."

So much for the element of surprise.

Xun steps forward, wrapping my wrists with cord. "Keep an eye on the rest of them."

He pulls me out of the makeshift room toward the back of the massive tent. A single cord is tied around the one that binds my wrists together and he tugs on it with his far hand, wrapping the other around my back to keep me close.

"What are you planning, Mulan?" he murmurs. "And don't try to convince me you're here for me. I know you're not."

I don't respond.

"I've brought you the jade dragon, Father," Xun announces, walking us into the room. Chen snaps the box shut and turns to face us.

"The concubine?"

"Surely you must recognize Lin Mulan, Father."

"This is your *bride*, my son?" Chen sounds surprised.

"I found her with Lanying. She didn't arrive here by accident—the emperor is likely nearby."

Chen steps over to us swiftly. "So, you're my son's new plaything—so kind of you to mention that earlier. Where is your emperor?"

"I haven't had the pleasure of meeting him." Technically, I'm still not supposed to know he's disguised as a general and waiting next to Keung for our signal.

"Probably for the best—we don't need you getting

emotional when we behead him. Is he on his way? He keeps coming for the gift I stole from him.

"Xun, go warn the others." He turns to his son. "I want a word with Miss Lin."

"No, Father. I will stay with Mulan and get answers for you. She is my bride, after all. You promised if I led your armies, I could have her. Let me find out what she knows."

"Fine. Find out what she knows, but don't get too comfortable—if we're stepping into battle, you need to be ready. You can enjoy her when we're done, and that foolish emperor is dead." He smiles, stepping around us. He picks up his box along the way. "Yan Liu will fall to us today, then on toward the other kingdoms."

Chen pauses, leaning over my shoulder. "I promised my son reign of Yan Liu. Today, you will become his queen...or concubine, up to you. Think carefully before you make your next move, Miss Lin."

Xun waits until he's out of range to speak.

"Tell me what you know, Mulan. I know you care for those people. The more I know now means the less people have to die when we confront them."

"Concubine?" I question.

"Mulan," he warns.

"Will you really keep me as a concubine, Xun? Knowing I'll never willingly be with you?"

"We'll discuss this later. Tell me what you know of his assault. I'm trying to help you."

"I know you're holding me prisoner, Xun. I know you've bound my wrists and offered me to your father as a pawn in his pathetic war to keep a treasure that isn't his.

"He's killing Yan Liu, Xun. The kingdom he's promised you—it's dying. Its people will never follow you—"

"They will with you at my side." Xun cuts me off, running a hand through his hair. "You're so stubborn, Mulan."

"You think you can fix all this by killing the emperor's army and installing yourself as a king to *my* people?" I rage. "You think I'll *ever* help you with this? You're mad, Xun. You've lost your mind."

"You'll come around." He walks away from me and I consider killing him, but I can't give away my position yet.

"I won't. Lock me up and turn me into your pet if you want, but I won't stand with you." I shove my wrists at him, showing him what he's done to me.

He must not have my sister, or else he would have used her against me already. At least that's one thing I don't have to worry about.

"Lover's quarrel?" the silver dragon steps in behind us. "Tsk. And here I thought I'd find you in the throes of passion."

"You knew you wouldn't." I sneer at her.

"We'll see when this is all over."

"Leave us, Lanying." Xun orders.

"Your father wants you. Bring the girl—he has a plan to draw out the emperor." She turns, hair flowing out behind her in a mass of curls.

"She takes quite a few liberties for being your father's *concubine*," I mutter as Xun leads me out a moment after Lanying is gone. He gives me a look that confirms I'm right about the silver dragon's status.

Xun walks us through the tent and back into the light. It's bright outside. I blink as my eyes adjust. One of the men standing watch over the entrance nods to the side, showing Xun where to go.

We walk to the edge of the camp where we first came in. Chen is waiting with a group of his men. Daiyu, Song, and Liling all stand in the middle. Thankfully, they aren't bound as I am.

"Time to draw them out," Chen proclaims as we get close. "Beat them."

"What?" Liling and I gasp at the same time. Xun protests on my behalf.

"We don't need to beat them to draw him out—"

"We'll spare your women, Xun." Chen waves his hand dismissively.

"Hung," Lanying addresses him in a seductive voice. "Perhaps there are other ways?"

"I thought you wanted to shred Miss Lin? Isn't that what you said?" Chen smirks as he calls her out. Xun glowers beside me and I'm sure he's saying vicious things to her through their connection.

"Your son does not wish to see his bride's friends hurt." She waves her hand at her king. "It is your choice."

"We can draw them out in other ways, Father—"

Xun stops speaking as I move next to him.

From my belt, I draw out my fan. The soldiers move quickly, raising their weapons to defend their master. They settle once they realize I only have a dancing fan in my bound hands.

I bow slightly, flipping the fan open. The dark color laced with sparkling gold catches their attention. Still bound, I twirl it once before waving it shut. I nod to the girls.

Slowly, they pull out the fans I gave them. They present them carefully, positioning themselves with hands on their hearts and wait for permission to dance with them.

No one suspects three of the four fans contain blades to be used against them.

"You wish to dance?" Chen asks.

"They will see us and come if that is what you

believe." I flip the fan open and hold it over the lower part of my face flirtatiously. "If you want us to be seen, this is how to do it, your highness."

Xun flinches as I call his father by his title.

"By all means then, entertain us."

I step forward, the others meeting me in the middle. The soldiers sit on boxes of supplies, weapons ready. I cast a long look at Daiyu and Liling, hoping they're ready.

Music starts somewhere, surprising me. It's the same lilting tune from before. It starts slow. We cover our faces, revealing them slowly.

The women of Yan Liu are trained in the arts of the fan the same way most men are trained in the warrior's way. It only takes a moment to fall into the same routine with each other, lifting and swirling our fans. My movements are stifled by the ropes around my wrist, but I get by, tilting at odd angles in an attempt to keep up with the girls.

Song starts singing along with the music, lifting and trilling her voice. The men don't know she's giving us cues —her notes changing just slightly from the original to indicate we should prepare ourselves. I'm not sure how she manages to communicate to us like this, but I wonder if that touch of dragon's blood in her has something to do with it.

The men who aren't busy watching for an oncoming

attack look transfixed upon us as we open and close our fans, moving them to the music.

Song's voice slides up and I know the moment is coming. We'll move as one, attacking the men next to us. Liling inches herself toward a box filled with rockets that she can set off as a signal for our men to rush into the encampment.

In the distance, blossoms fall off the trees on the wind. Tiny pink petals float toward us. The wind is peaceful—a calming presence before the battle. We'll likely die before the men reach us, so I hold onto the image as Song's voice shifts, activating us.

We move quickly out of the center toward the closest soldier and flip our blades out. I slice the man's throat leaving him gaping at me. He tips forward, clutching at his throat.

Spinning the fan, I cut myself free, nicking my palm, and attack another man.

The group is on their feet, rushing toward us with weapons drawn. Daiyu shifts, towering over the men in her dragon form. She surprises them and manages to burn a few before they can get out of her way.

Turning, I cut into a man who ran up behind me. Several men lay in Liling's wake. She runs toward the rockets and sends one up to signal our men.

Song attempts to block for her but is quickly captured

—I'm thankful we didn't give her a weapon that could be used against her. She bites down on the man's arm as I transform. My shriek sounds as I lumber toward Liling to keep the soldiers away from her while she works.

Xun shouts at me before transforming, begging me not to fight him. I burn as many men as I can without harming Song, stopping only as Xun tries to face me.

The rocket goes off, plunging into the sky and exploding. Daiyu lets out a terrifying scream as the surviving men of the group use their dragon teeth to bite into her.

Suddenly, we're surrounded by dragons—our own. The general drops his shield gift and unveils an army of men transforming around him. Chen's men are taken by surprise as they rush to his aid.

The war is about to end.

Chapter 22

A PIERCING SCREECH FILLS THE SKY, RATTLING ME TO my bones. My scales prickle on my body as the cries of two armies of dragons fills the air. Song struggles against her captor as he pulls her away from the crowd, blade to her throat.

Keung lands behind the man holding the young girl, shifting quietly. In his human form, he walks up behind him, blade ready. He doesn't even notice my lieutenant. He falls to the ground as Keung pulls the blade across his throat. I see him instruct Song to run to the general who paces in his dragon form at the back of the army, waiting to make his move to take back the black jade blossom after retreating for his safety.

I claw at a dragon, angling my head so I can watch Keung and Song. The dragon hisses at me and I breathe fire back, having enough of this petty squabble.

Song runs and our weyr makes sure she gets there safely. Still too injured, Ning waits with the general, his only job to protect the young girl.

Keung transforms back to his red scales and makes his way to me. I fight my way past two dragons, meeting Keung on the outside of the fight. He quickly transforms and I follow so we can speak in our human forms.

"Are you okay?"

"Chen is here—he's got the black jade blossom with him in a box that glows when you open it—he's Xun's father," I blurt.

"Fantastic. No wonder he has that over-inflated ego— he thinks he's a prince."

"That would be it." I nod.

"Do you have a plan?" he asks, waiting to follow my lead.

"Aside from burning them all? Not really."

"So, we see where this takes us?" He grabs my hand.

"We see where this takes us," I confirm.

Keung kisses my hand, then notices Xun in his white dragon form watching us. He wraps his arms around me and tips me back into a kiss. Before lifting me up, he turns his head, looking directly at the white dragon to make his point—I'm his.

He pulls me back up. "Ready?"

We transform at the same time, diving back into the

fray. Some of the dragons fight on the ground, while others have taken to the sky. Keung and I lift off and do as much damage to the enemy as possible.

My fire lights up tents and supplies, destroying them while Keung carefully smashes the rest of the rockets, preventing them from being used against us. The land becomes a maze of fire—thankfully no one is trying to navigate it. I saw the soldiers move the concubines when the battle started—I'll find them later.

I swoop down, searching for enemy dragons. Wei battles a particularly large dragon and I race toward him to help. Together, we force him back—he nearly made it beyond our line to get to the general. Keung dives down, finishing him as we hold him back.

Wei moves on to another fight as Keung glides into my view. He latches onto a darker red dragon from Chen's forces, spinning in the air with the monstrous soldier.

I engage with a smaller dragon that doesn't stand a chance against me. He falls easy prey to my fire, and as I turn my attention back to Keung, I notice the general has joined the fray.

As I turn to find my next fight, I come face-to-face with Chen in his dragon form. He roars at me, exposing his rows of sharp teeth. Clutched in one foot is the box containing the black jade blossom.

He jerks his head back, preparing to fight with me.

His other front foot snakes across the space between us, swiping at my exposed neck and chest. His claws run deep and blood drips from my scales to the world below. I scream in pain and annoyance.

Eyeing the box, I work out a plan to get it. If I can distract him and take it from him, my sole job will be to get as far from the battle as possible and not stop until I've reached the emperor's palace. I don't want to leave the others behind to fight, but I can't risk waiting to hide it.

Using my tail, I tap the underside of his bottom foot, hoping to draw his attention. He kicks at it, not taking his eyes off of me. Turning, he uses his wing to try to knock me off balance, but I build my fire in response. His dragon eyes widen, knowing what I'm about to do. Chen drops, avoiding my fiery blast. It hits one of his soldiers beyond him.

Looking up, the general takes notice of Chen. I cry to him, signaling. He lifts up in the air and takes Chen on for himself. I rush to help but Xun's cloud-white body slams into me, tearing off scales as we hit.

I tumble over him in the sky. We fall, crashing to the ground. I take the brunt of the hit, slamming into the dirt and rolling over tents. Xun pins me down, towering over me. His chest rises and falls heavily as he stares down at me. It seems like a dynasty before he focuses again, rearing his head back and striking at me.

I move my head to the side and his nose slams into the ground. Xun snorts angrily and snaps at me, teeth just short of connecting. I wriggle under him, trying to work a limb loose so I can fight back. When I can't, I bare my teeth, ready to bite.

Xun shifts, avoiding my strike. He slams his foot against me in retribution, knocking the wind out of me. Baring my teeth again, I threaten him. He growls in return, prompting me to scream at him in anger. Xun hovers over me as we battle with our dragon voices.

Just as I consider shifting to escape, Xun is flung away from me. A bright flash of red races by, saving me from the white dragon's hold.

Keung roars viciously at Xun. Ordinarily, I might not mind two men fighting over me, but it's quite different in dragon form than in our human bodies.

I move to team up with Keung but the cry behind me stops me. Her fire sparks along my back, snapping and tingling as she demands my attention. Slowly, I turn, finding the silver dragon hovering next to me.

She lands, slowly walking over to me across the dirt and grass as if a war wasn't happening around us. She doesn't look to the left or right, just locks gazes with me and moves.

Her silver scales shine in the sunlight. Blood coats one of her sides, dripping to the ground as she walks, though she acts as if she doesn't notice. Lines from her interrogation stretch across her body, more prominent now than before.

Lanying tips her head at me, looking my scales up and down. I feel her intense gaze across the distance as it seers into my scales. I'm acutely aware of the hole in my side as blood trickles out, inching its way over my skin.

Dipping her tail into a pool of blood, she uses it to draw a small circle on the ground, reminding me of her threat. She means to kill me.

Behind me, Keung attacks Xun. I block out their battles cries to focus on the silver dragon—her posturing can only mean her impending attack will be brutal. Beyond her in the sky, the general is entangled with Chen —the soldiers on both sides come to their defense as the black jade blossom waits for its fate to be decided.

Slowly, the silver dragon flaps her wings. The beat pulses the grass around her, waving it with every movement. She carefully rises into the air and waits for me to join her.

With Keung battling on the ground and the general fighting to the death in the sky, I hover somewhere in the middle, waiting to be attacked by a middle-aged concubine who somehow managed to control at least part of what her king is doing.

Suddenly, she jerks her head around me, looking beyond where I fly—she must be communicating with Xun through their gift. She shakes her head, finally looking back at me with narrow eyes.

If Keung takes down Xun, the general removes Chen, and I take out the silver dragon, we have a chance at winning the war and returning the black jade blossom to the emperor's palace to restore Yan Lui and the surrounding kingdoms who benefit from its powers. I slow my breathing, focusing in on my destiny.

Her dragon form is sleek as it arches through the sky. She shoots straight up, arching back down on me in an overhead attack. I twist, rolling so when she latches onto me with her claws, she's thrown off by my sudden roll.

She falls forward, losing her grip on me. Using my back legs, I kick her as she stumbles, forcing her nearly to the ground.

When she turns back, unbridled anger ripples off her in waves—the black jade blossom's power over the river looks like child's play compared to what's rolling off the silver dragon.

Her movements are slow once again and she patiently moves like a serpent, back and forth. It's the last time I'll ever see her clearly.

Lanying attacks. Her strikes are chaotic and painful.

She rips and tears any piece of dragon flesh she can find. In return, I fight back, maiming her as best I can.

Each time my teeth sink into her, I pull them back immediately only to strike again. When I was a child, I witnessed a dog fight in the streets near the Center—they appeared tame compared to this vicious assault.

Xun's screech fills the air, though I'm not sure if it's directed at us or if Keung is gaining the upper hand. Lanying appears to have no trouble going against Xun's wishes to kill me in battle. Until now, it had appeared she might care for the boy, but she only has revenge on her mind now.

We claw at each other, both dropping in the sky, only to separate and fly higher to get the advantage and nose-dive again when we engage. Exhaustion is building up inside of me, making it hard to create my fire. Lanying seems almost resistant to my flame, but it's pure willpower on her part as scales melt off her body.

Behind me, a dragon falls out of the sky, collapsing heavily on the ground below. From the corner of my eye, I see Keung and Xun tearing each other apart.

Scaring me, Jinhai appears by my side, barely able to fly with his injuries. He aligns himself with me and prepares to take on the silver dragon.

Together, we strike. She fights back, hitting us both

with her claws. I bite down on her foot so hard, it nearly detaches, rending it useless in the battle.

Jinhai distracts her, but she takes his aggression as an invitation to focus her full attention on killing my brother in front of me. The silver dragon slams into him, but he uses the same trick I did, rolling as she attaches herself to him.

They topple over each other, crashing into the ground. Jinhai immediately rolls away, flopping down in the grass as his body succumbs to the pain and injuries he's endured in this battle and the last.

I pin the silver dragon to the ground as Xun had done to me. Unlike my childhood friend, I have no mercy and don't question my actions. She screams, hissing fire at me as I melt her face away. Through my flames, I can barely see her scales fall off her skull, dripping to the ground below her. When I'm sure she's no longer a threat, I release her, jerking her charred body away from me as I get up.

So much for painting my body with my own blood.

Jinhai shifts into his human form and I grip him in my claws, lifting off to carry him to where Song and Ning wait in the distance. He reaches for me to keep me with him when I set him down, but I can't stay—I have to fight.

Dragon carcasses and human corpses lie scattered on the ground between the hill and the general. Soldiers that transformed into their human bodies have been seized and shackled so they can't shift and reenter the battle. Several of our men guard them from being broken free.

From what I can tell, we have the upper hand. Now, we just need to kill Chen and return the black jade blossom to the emperor. I dart toward the enemy king, flame ready.

Chapter 23

Fire rages, covering the entire ground beneath the general and Chen. The scent of burning dragon scales fills the air. The heat is intense enough to feel through my protective scales.

Smoke makes it hard to see. In my human form, it would be enough to suffocate me. I blink, trying to clear my vision as I approach the brawl.

Dragons crash into each other as they fight against others. Through the smoke, it looks like a flock of birds has risen into the air and collide when one turns the group without warning.

I find my mark, a flash of Chen's emerald catching my eye as he tangles with the general. He nearly drops the box with our prize, sending it into the fires below. *I wonder what would happen if it fell into the flames?*

Taking a lesson from the silver dragon, I move slowly

toward my intended victim. I try to keep from drawing attention to myself.

Flying as low as I dare, I endure the heat of the flames as they lick at my exposed underside. Most off the enemy dragons that remain take no notice of me, busy in their battles with my weyr.

It's agony moving so slowly while also hoovering over the flames that I'm sure are attempting to singe my scales, but I have to be precise in my attack. Getting the box away from Chen before incinerating him won't be easy, but I have to do it.

Wei spots me. He tracks my path, turning his head to face Chen and the emperor-disguised-as-a-military-leader. My friend dips down as the fire spreads below us pushing our soldiers with their captives further back.

I nod toward the enemy leader and hold out my injured front foot, twitching my claws together. Wei nods. Together, we will approach Chen and defeat him. Wei will retrieve the box—likely at a very high price—while I face the enemy king head-on in hopes of destroying him.

I fly next to Wei, aligning myself with him. He looks at me and nods, closing his eyes—*some type of goodbye?*

One of us will likely not escape the attack. Since he's the one with the black jade blossom, I'm hoping Wei will be the one to escape. I'll risk my life to make sure he is.

The moment Wei has the box, I'm going to attack

Chen and force him to the ground to burn in the fires below—I'll go with him if my flames won't suffice to stop him.

We fly together, rising up high enough that should we be noticed, he can still dip down and take Chen by surprise. I picture Ming as we move—imagine her freedom once the black jade blossom has been returned. She'll never get the hairpin I found for her. It will burn with me.

Wei branches off, tossing me a look. I hover, waiting for him to get around. I picture my parents who still don't know Jinhai and I both survived the attack on the Center —at least they didn't have the hope of their daughter surviving only to be told she died in battle. It will save them a little heartache.

Beyond Chen and the general, Wei turns, waiting for my signal. Jinhai's face flashes in my mind. My twin will be alright—he'll hold our family together.

I glance behind me, taking a final look at Keung. I regret leaving him, but there's no way I'll survive this battle. Even if I do, I'll be shattered and broken, far too gone for anything more than lying in a bed suffering. He fights against Xun, both men exhausted and badly injured.

Keung swings around, catching my eye. He pulls back his head in shock and cries out to me, seeing I'm about to rush to his father's aid. His pleas can't stop what I'm about to do.

I turn, nodding slightly to Wei.

We move at the same time. I slam into Chen, knocking him away from the weakening general. Surprised, Chen takes a moment to move out of my way, allowing me to move him far enough to give us an advantage.

I'll end you.

Chen hisses at me, looking away only when he hears Xun's warning shriek. He glances at his son, then back to me with narrowed eyes.

Clutching the box tighter, he flies toward me, flapping his wings strongly to create gushes of air that stoke the fire below us. I rear my head back, trying to look like I'm building my fire. He pulls back, ducking his head. Chen's eyes close just enough that I can dart forward without him seeing me and bite deeply into his shoulder.

Behind him, Wei approaches completely unnoticed by our enemy. The dragons around us form a circle, preventing Chen's men from coming to his aid. They fight viciously to protect us and give us our best chance at surviving.

The general swoops at Chen, knocking him off guard again. I use my blaze to sear his back haunch and tail. He roars, turning on me. Before I can react, Chen whips back, biting deeply into the general's neck. Our emperor roars in pain and I lunge at Chen, trying to take on his wrath.

The general bleeds more than he should—I'm worried about his survival. He sinks lower in the sky, unable to hold himself up.

Xun and Keung cry out at the same time. I can't afford to look, but I pray they both survive.

Chen races toward me but I don't veer. Colliding with him could send both of us to the ground and its fiery graves or it could give Wei the chance he needs to take the box.

The general calls to Chen, trying to distract him—and save me in the process—but if the general dies, Yan Liu may not recover. It *certainly* won't recover if the black jade blossom is lost.

Angry, Chen focuses only on me. I'm his target—if I can keep his attention, the black jade blossom will be ours. Wei starts to make his move, tolerating the burning fire beneath him as he makes his way to the box slowly.

I rush toward Chen. He clenches his jaw, preparing to lock into battle with me. Rotating his foot, he holds the box closer to his chest, making it hard for Wei to steal it away from him. If I can get him to drop it, Wei can catch it in the air.

My bite is hard, but as Chen moves, it sinks into his chest instead of his front leg. He barely grunts, miraculously avoiding the piercing shriek I know he must be holding in. He slashes at me, catching my shoulder—it's going to hurt when I shift.

I lunge at him again, this time ripping a hole in his side. It gushes blood, but I had to sacrifice my front leg for the cause. Chen rips at me again, breaking my scales—possibly my bones—and sends such horrific pain through my body that the world goes fuzzy. I try to move it but can't.

I build my fire, hurling it at him. His scales start to melt but he doesn't hesitate to rush *at* me instead of away. Chen slams into me, knocking the fire out in my mouth. He bites down, taking a chunk out of my lower neck above my injured leg. I may never have use of the arm again in my human form.

I summon my fire again, prepared to wield it against him when I see Wei positioning himself under the enemy leader. My lungs burn with each breath I take. Not even the wind helps to cool my scales down from the scalding fire below us.

Chen swings around as the general approaches and slams into him with his tail. The general falls back, colliding with one of our soldiers.

Managing to stay hidden underneath Chen in his blind spot, Wei waits, enduring the fire crackling up at him. If he can get the box with the black jade blossom, I need to keep Chen from chasing him. I have one chance—my back up plan is to drag him into the fire with me.

Wei grasps for the box, knocking it from Chen's grasp. The enemy leader growls, diving down to catch it. He grabs the box, clutching it to his chest. Wei failed.

Chen targets him, but I won't lose our last chance. I scream, flying for him. Chen turns just in time for me to collide with him.

Throwing fire at him, I scald his scales as we dive straight down into the fire. I rip his wing, preventing him from saving himself. It tears under my claws, ripping like the thick fabric of a tent against an enemy blade, jerking and shattering.

I try to knock the box from his front foot as we fall but can't manage with my injuries—perhaps the black jade blossom can survive the fires. It's survived so many other things throughout the dynasties, so why not this?

I'm locked in a free-fall with Chen. Neither of us can stop. The fires race up around us as we plummet down between the flames.

The ground draws nearer. I want to close my eyes to avoid my own death but I can't. I watch Chen as he panics.

The flames burn me. Agony unlike anything I've ever known presents itself, taunting me. I wonder if this is what it was like for the dragons I burned in battle—no, their deaths were faster.

I consider shifting if the collision with the ground doesn't kill me—it will take longer to burn as a dragon and I don't want to prolong my pain. But I also have to worry about Chen's survival—I may not have a choice if I want to ensure his death.

I suck in a breath of air, preparing for impact. It won't be long.

Chen flips me, pulling at my injured front leg so that he rests on top of me, leaving me to take the brunt of the fall. Before I can move to flip him, he shifts to his human form, making it impossible for me to grab him.

Suddenly, water flies everywhere, quenching the flames. Chen managed to open the box and use the black jade's powers to put out the fire around us in a large circle.

We slam into the ground and everything goes black.

Chapter 24

I BLINK, TRYING TO SEE THROUGH THE SMOKE AND steam. Chen sits up with the black jade blossom in his hand. It's stunning.

The large flower covers his palm, black petals draping over to the side in an elegant way. The crystal effect makes it sparkle, catching every inch of the fire surrounding us.

If I can trust what I saw, the water flowed out of Chen to put out the flames beneath us. Much like the emperor pays a price to activate the black jade blossom, Chen had to give of himself to put out the flames, literally drawing water from within.

I snap my head up as Chen starts to sit. He glares at me and begins to shift, blossom in his claws.

I have one chance of survival.

To the side, a man's bones rest, having been eatten by

the flames. Little remains of him. His sword, however, waits for me.

I dive for it as Chen adopts his scales once more, running toward me with fire ready. He will burn me, but I'll take him down with me.

I swing as he comes within range. The foolish man should have burned me from a distance but he hasn't seen my new weapon.

I plunge the sword into his chest and he shrieks. Xun's father withers in front of me but doesn't drop the black jade blossom.

He shifts to his human form, trying to use it against me. A stream of water trickles out, dripping onto the ground in front of him, much smaller than the pool of blood I've drawn from him.

Chen tries to shift again but isn't strong enough. He falls to his knees. I pull the sword from the ground where it fell when he shifted and move toward him dangerously.

I don't want to kill him. He's my childhood friend's father. I knew him growing up. He came to my village, he talked to my father, he was a part of my life for however short a time it may have been.

But Chen is also the enemy.

Chen tried to kill us all.

He tries one more time to activate the black jade blossom, this time succeeding in unleashing a force of water so hard it knocks me over and puts out enough of the fire still surrounding us that our men can see his final breath.

My arm can't be used. It hangs limply at my side. Tears stream down my face as I take an uneasy step forward, knees nearly giving out.

The blossom nearly glows in his hand, protesting it's use as he tries to force it one more time. Chen's eyes flutter open and shut as he watches me, breathing heavily.

I hold the sword out to him.

"Surrender!" I demand.

He moves and I can tell he's going to try to shift.

"Don't do it, Chen! Don't make your son watch you die!"

Chen opens his mouth to speak, blood trickling out. The wound in his chest leaks more blood, leaving him in a dark pool.

"You can take this from me," he says, struggling to get his words out, "but my army will never bow to you. They'll continue this war. My son will rise up and end Yan Liu. You will submit to his rule."

"No, actually, Yan Liu will go on to thrive and forget you and this entire war ever happened," I contradict him. "You will be nothing once again, Chen Hung. You will be as meaningless as you have always been."

He staggers forward, blood dripping from his boot. Raising his arm, he kneels, touching the ground with his open hand. The black jade blossom glows, sparking tiny black dots from it as he attempts to tap into its power and draw water from the earth.

He murmurs something, glaring at me. Chen tips his head back as I stumble toward him, prepared to stop him.

Before I can reach him, the ground shudders beneath us as a dragon lands nearby. Chen keeps his focus on me, narrowing his eyes. Pointing the sword, I prepare to run.

Chen's hand falls in front of him, separating from his wrist. The black jade blossom tumbles out of his open fingers, falling away from the growing pool of blood.

Dots of red cover my kimono, already stained with soot and singed by the fire. I blink as I realize he's lost his hand. Beyond him, a fan clatters on the ground, blades still out.

I strike, plunging the sword into his chest and out of his back. He looks up at me, blood dripping from his lips. Slowly, he falls to the side. Death comes quickly for him— far faster than it should.

I step back, resting deeply on my heels. Liling runs up —she must have cut Chen's hand off with the fan. I blink.

I succumb to the pain and drop.

Chapter 25

The breeze rustles the red silk curtains to the right. Light shines through them, dazzling the entire room with its brightness. The breeze sweeps across my cheek as I try to focus.

Lanterns hang in the corners, their tassels rustling with the wind. A string of smaller lanterns crosses from one end of the ceiling too another.

White and black screens fill one wall leading to the closed door. I breathe in. Opposite, the bed sits against the wall—this one covered in artistic images telling the story of the history of the province and how the dragons came to be.

I blink my eyes closed, still trying to wake up.

My mouth is dry like I haven't had water in a dynasty. Everything aches, but I can move my arm that I thought was injured.

Light streams into the room, dancing in odd patterns as the silk curtains shift again. I groan, trying to figure out where I am.

"Good morning." Daiyu chuckles from somewhere in my blind spot.

"Stay down." Song appears at my shoulder, gently placing her hands on me to restrain me and prevent me from sitting up.

"What happened?" My voice is worse than I anticipated it to be.

"You killed Chen," Daiyu says.

"After Liling chopped his hand off," Song adds.

Dust sparkles in the air. I look up and find the entire ceiling is made of draped fabric. It's the most elegant thing I've seen in my life.

"Where—"

"The palace," Song replies softly. "We've been here for an entire day. You've been in and out, so you probably don't remember."

I shoot upright despite her attempts to stop me. "Did we get it back? Is the black jade blossom safe—?"

"Calm down, Mulan. It's safe." Daiyu chuckles again and sits on the bed next to me.

To the side sits a low table with bowls and food. Some of it appears to be eaten—I assume the girls taking care of me haven't left my side.

"Your family has been summoned—they should be here soon."

"How exactly did I get here? And why can I move my arm again?"

"We all had a hand in that," Daiyu answers. "The general—who is apparently the *emperor*—Keung, and I were able to heal you with the help of the black jade blossom and Keung's gift. Song sewed you up. Your brother didn't leave your side until we arrived and forced him out."

"He's been here most of the time, but he wasn't allowed to sleep here since we've been staying with you. He should be here soon though now that the sun is up." Song busies herself checking my injuries.

"You'll have some nasty scars, Mulan, but you'll survive." Daiyu's words are soft.

"I can live with that." I try to smile at her. "Keung and Xun?"

"Both are injured—Xun nearly fatally, but we saved him too when we were done with you," Daiyu explains. "Keung carried you all the way back here—wouldn't let anyone else touch you."

"Jinhai was livid." Song giggles. "But he was in no shape to carry you—he could barely fly himself."

She looks up suddenly. "Oh, but he's okay. He's better now. Ning is healing well too."

Song blushes as I lay back against the pillow.

A sharp breath of air from the doorway pulls our attention. Keung sags against the door frame. "You're awake."

Daiyu and Song stand without saying anything, hurrying toward the door. They nod to the prince as they leave.

Keung watches me for a moment before shutting the door behind him. Laying back against my pillow, I watch him make his way toward me.

He's clothed in the same red as his scales with golden accents on his shoulders. His robes crash around his feet as he walks, sleeves only revealing the tips of his fingers. He's breath-taking.

"May I?" he asks as he approaches.

I close my eyes and dip my head toward the bed next to me. He turns and I notice the intricate dragon embroidered on the back of his robe in golden threads with jewels sparkling in the early morning sunlight.

Glancing down, I find I'm in a similar kimono of jade with intricate detailing on the sleeves. My hair shifts over my arms as I turn to face him better.

Keung reaches out, fingers dancing over a strand of my hair. He pulls it through his fingers several times before making eye contact with me.

"He's alright," Keung starts. I blink in confusion—that

was not what I expected him to say. "Xun—he's injured, but he's alive."

My face goes slack. My heart wants to be concerned for the boy, but my head tells me not to be.

"It's okay to still care about him, Mulan. He was a big part of your life," Keung assures me. "He's stable thanks to Daiyu and the palace physicians. He'll spend the rest of his days in prison, though. We can't trust him even if we think he's changed."

"His father told me Xun will carry on his war," I confirm. "I believe him."

"The fighting isn't over, Mulan. There's still more to come, but now that we have the black jade blossom back, we hope to put an end to it in the next few months."

Keung reaches over to touch my hair with both of his hands. He leans in to look at me—I wish he'd kiss me already. He smiles knowingly and pulls back slightly.

"You were magnificent out there, Mulan. My father is very impressed with you."

"And what about *you*? Did I impress *you*?"

"To be fair, I'm more impressed with your kissing skills, but yes, you impressed me out there too. Although, I was ready to kill you myself with some of those impulsively dangerous decisions you made."

"You would have made them, too," I protest as the

curtains move again and cast a red hue over Keung's face and shoulder accents.

"I really want to lecture you for almost dying, but..." he pauses. "You saved us, Mulan. You killed Chen and got our kingdom's life source back."

His expression is so strange as he stares at me. With eyebrows furrowed and mouth pursed, I want nothing more than to lean up and part his lips. I reach up, running my hand along his cheek.

"Mulan!" Jinhai yells, slamming the door open. We both jump but refuse to pull away from each other. We turn, staring at my brother with my hand still on Keung's cheek as he leans over me.

My twin looks taken aback. "What is this? I said no to this."

With eyebrows raised and fists balled, he stalks over to us.

"No, actually you didn't," Keung corrects him. He grins with satisfaction. "I was your commanding officer— you couldn't say anything to me. And now I'm your prince —do you dare tell me I can't do something?"

Jinhai doesn't back down. "I do. *Back off.*"

My jaw drops open and I can't hold back my grin. Keung's expression matches mine. The prince reaches up to pull my hand from his cheek and brings it to his lips, kissing my fingers until I think Jinhai will turn from red to purple.

Much like Keung, Jinhai is dressed formally in blue silk robes that flow like Keung's. Dragon scales drip down the sides of his long sleeves in silver thread.

"Why is everyone so dressed up?" I ask.

"Oh," Keung murmurs, turning back to me. "Today we are honoring our soldiers for returning the black jade blossom to the emperor. We're dressed for the ceremony."

"And exactly how long have I been dressed for the ceremony?" I ask, glancing at my intricate sleeves.

"You're *not* dressed for the ceremony." Keung chuckles. "The woman responsible for saving Yan Liu will be dressed far more decadently before gracing the palace steps to be honored.

"Besides," he leans in to whisper, "There are other reasons you need to be dressed up for this."

The corner of his lip tugs up in a flirtatious snarl making Jinhai gag. Keung chuckles victoriously. "*Oh, Jinhai.* I'm going to enjoy this."

"If you weren't the emperor's son, I'd strangle you," Jinhai comments.

"You only think you can speak to me that way because I love your sister." Keung leans forward to snuggle his forehead against mine, still staring down my brother to harass him.

"You realize our mother is a dragon, right?" Jinhai announces. "If you thought Mulan could do some damage, wait until she finds out you've been secretly dating her daughter all this time and nearly got her killed in a war she was never supposed to be in."

"Oh please, Jinhai. Parents love me." Keung sits up, sweeping his hand out to the side.

"He *is* a charmer," I confirm. "But if you two are going to keep this up, you should probably take it out to the hallway so I can get dressed for this ceremony."

Keung swings back around to look at me, a pout on his face. "But we didn't even get to kiss yet..."

"You decided to waste our time talking to my brother instead..." I shrug. "Now get out."

I poke Keung until he stands and I motion for both of them to leave. Swinging my feet around, I touch the cold marble floor. I stand, rounding the bed and walk to the open window which turns out to be a door to a balcony as I wait for the girls to return and help me dress.

# Chapter 26

THE AIR IS THE PERFECT TEMPERATURE AS THE blossoms fall from the trees on the breeze. I hold my hands in front of me, hidden in long red sleeves. My navy dress with red accents reflects the emperor and his son perfectly as I stand by Keung's side.

Proudly, he watches as his father addresses the province, telling the tale of how Chen was vanquished. Keung bumps into me each time his father says my name.

I left my hair down for the ceremony and it tickles against my chin and neck as the wind moves it. It brushes over my bare shoulders where the sleeves have been cut out on top. Keung's hair moves too, looking glorious.

From my place on the landing atop the palace steps, I can see my family. My father is holding Ming back who looks like she wants to run the entire flight of golden steps to me and my twin.

Jinhai stands as tall as possible at my other side, Wei, Ning, and several others to be honored standing beside him. They're proud to be acknowledged by the emperor but not nearly as proud as I am of them and their sacrifices.

Ning leans heavily against Wei and Jinhai for support, but he insists on standing on his own. His parents watch from their place next to my family.

Daiyu, Liling, and Song stand on the emperor's other side, waiting for their turn to be mentioned.

"—without their quick thinking, the black jade blossom and the battle would have been lost," the emperor says. "They have saved us all.

"And one day, when my son takes over, we will be lucky enough to have these sons and daughters of Yan Liu there to help and guide him. Today, we honor our dragons and soldiers who fought valiantly. Tomorrow, we *follow* them."

The crowd bows deeply to us.

My father's eyes fill with tears that shine brightly enough for me to see from this distance. Mother looks happy enough to burst at the seams—I can tell she's fighting the urge to shift and fly.

Each of us is called by name and the emperor gives an account of our heroics. He gives each soldier the highest promotion and an invitation to serve on the council of the palace during his reign. Keung seconds it, asking them to serve with him once it's his turn to lead. All accept.

"The battle is over," the emperor announces, "but the war goes on. Do not let your guards down. Yan Liu is a province of peace. We will help to restore Zhao Wu and its rightful emperor, and in time, help to restore the surrounding kingdoms as well in hopes of peace among us all once again."

Keung takes my hand in his. My father notices and pales. I smile and he relaxes. He'll enjoy meeting Keung this afternoon once the ceremony is over.

Ribbons and fabric blow on the breeze in bold colors of the province. Around us, lanterns float into the sky with their tassels dangling behind them.

Music fills the air as a dancing fabric dragon bursts out of a door on the ground with the crowd to celebrate our victorious return and streamers burst into the air.

Confetti drifts around us, nearly creating a curtain between the people on the steps and the crowd of people below.

Keung turns and kisses me publicly for the first time.

The prince walks me back to my room in the palace after

dinner with our parents and the other soldiers who were honored. We slow as we reach my door.

"Coming in for a bit?" I ask.

He offers me a smoldering smile and follows behind me. When the door closes, he reaches up and places a hand against the doorframe. Keung leans into me.

"Now that we can finally court publicly, I think I can get used to this." He bends to kiss me, wrapping his free arm around my waist.

I lift up on my toes, pulling him closer to me. His lips roam over my jaw, my neck, my shoulder until I sigh and pull back to watch him.

"Come sit with me?" he asks, gesturing past the table to a pile of pillows meant to act as a seat near the window.

I let him guide me over, my hand in his, and sit beside him. He watches me closely and I feel a blush creep into my cheeks.

"Still blushing around me, I see. Shouldn't you be over that by now? I'd hope you're comfortable with me, Mulan, after all that we've been through."

He leans in to kiss me again. I giggle but it only encourages him.

"Are you sure you want me, Keung? After all this?" I fight to hold still and not launch myself at him.

"Of course I want you. I've wanted you since you found me in the field that day—which I keep telling you.

You're the most fearsome woman I've ever met—you inspire and awe me—and you're also the most beautiful."

I glance down, running a hand over the scars on my arm.

"Maybe I *was*—"

"You *are*, Mulan," he corrects me, grabbing my hand. He pulls it roughly to his lips. "You are stunning."

"I'm glad you'll overlook my scars..."

"Your scars are what I love most, Mulan. They boast of what you did to get to me. There's nothing more beautiful than that, my love. And this is only the beginning of our story."

I can't help myself. I attack him, knocking him over.

He can stop my kisses whenever he'd like—I'll leave it up to him.

ACKNOWLEDGEMENTS

Thanks so much for coming with me on Mulan's journey! This project is a bit of a new take for me and involves some tropes I *never* thought I'd write in, but I'm glad I got to play with this book.

I hope you enjoyed Mulan and Keung's story as much as I enjoyed writing it!

Special thanks to the one instrumental song I had on replay for most of this book—you helped me survive the long writing days and get in the right headspace for this Asian-inspired novel! I'll give the song a shout out on the world portal page for Mulan Dragon Shifter on my website if you want to check it out!

If you loved the story as much as I did, send me an email or direct message and let me know so we can gush over it together—feel free to giggle if you picked the right ship or yell if I broke your heart because your ship sank hard.

Special thanks to Jess and Danielle for all of your help with Mulan Dragon Shifter!

Thank you to Alexis for being awesome.

And to you, oh lovely reader, thank you for coming on this journey with me. I don't write dragons or shifters often, but this has been a fun world for me to live in—especially since I'm stuck waiting for the next season of My Dear Cold-Blooded King to come out on Webtoon!

Be sure to hit up my website for more from the world of Mulan Dragon Shifter!

Stay inspired!

-K.M. Robinson

WORLD PORTALS

Ready to learn exclusive facts about Mulan Dragon Shifter and other K.M. Robinson Series?

World Portals are now available on www. kmrobinsonbooks.com

Learn behind the scenes facts, watch videos, play games, check out our book filters, find out where to get bonus scenes, view fan art, and get access to other secrets we've hidden away inside the World Portals on the website.

The World Portals are constantly changing and information is being taken away and added all the time, so check back frequently for new content!

ABOUT THE AUTHOR

K.M. Robinson is a storyteller who creates new worlds both in her writing and in her fine arts conceptual photography. She is a marketing, branding and social media strategy educator who is recognized at first sight by her very long hair. She is a creative who focuses on photography, videography, couture dress making, and writing to express the stories she needs to tell. She almost always has a camera within reach. Visit her at her website: www.kmrobinsonbooks.com

CONNECT ON SOCIAL MEDIA

facebook.com/kmrobinsonbooks

instagram.com/kmrobinsonbooks

twitter.com/kmrobinsonbooks

youtube.com/kmrobinsonbooks

Get free books and excerpts of other K.M. Robinson books at excerpt.kmrobinsonbooks.com

The Legends Chronicles

Along Came A Spider: A Prequel Novelette

And They'll Come Home: A Prequel Novelette

The Archives of Jack Frost Series

The Revolution of Jack Frost

The Redemption of Jack Frost (coming soon)

Stealing Steam Series

Book One: Lions and Lamps

Book Two: Pistons and Prisoners

Book Three: Railcars and Rulers

Top Hats and Telegraphs: A Prequel Novella

The Complete Series Boxset/Omnibus with Vambraces and
Victories: an exclusive bonus novella

Virtually Sleeping Beauty: A Novella Retelling

**The Goose Girl and The Artificial: A Novella
Retelling**

The Sinking: A Little Mermaid Novella Retelling

Cindrill: A Cinderella Assassin Novella Retelling

Sugarcoated: A Hansel and Gretel's Witch Novella Retelling

Blood Is Silent: A Red Riding Hood Circus Aerialist Retelling

JADED: BOOK ONE OF THE JADED DUOLOGY

Her father failed in his mission to take control from the Commander, a defeat that has cost Jade her life. She will die as punishment. Now she belongs to the Commander's son—as his wife. Knowing his intent is to quietly kill her in revenge, Jade's every move is calculated to survive—until she learns her death ensures the safety of her father and her entire town.

Roan doesn't want to kill Jade, but once his family isolates her from her father and community, his only choice is to go through with the plan. Jade doesn't make it easy as she tries to sway him into falling for her. Each misstep makes him question his cause. Each moment makes every decision harder, but the Commander won't allow him to fail.

One chooses life. One chooses death. In the midst of the chaos, only one will succeed.

Now available!
Learn more about The Jaded Duology at
jadedinfo.kmrobinsonbooks.com

Goldilocks wasn't naive. She was sent on a mission and Dov Baer is her new target.

When Auluria tricks the Baers into letting her into their home, they have no idea she's actually been sent by the enemy to destroy them. Intent on gathering information for her cousin to hand over to the Society seeking to destroy all of the rebel factions—including her own—she's willing to sacrifice Dov Baer to save her people...until she realizes her cousin lied to her.

Now that she's seen who Dov truly is, she has to decide between staying loyal to her only remaining family or protecting the man she's falling for. If her allegiances are discovered, either side could destroy her—assuming the Society doesn't get her first

Available now!
Learn more about The Golden Trilogy at goldeninfo.
kmrobinsonbooks.com

THE SIREN WARS: BOOK ONE OF THE SIREN WARS SAGA

War has hovered around the kingdom of Scylla for generations ever since the original sirens left the mer collection generations ago after nearly drowning the human prince. Over the years, select mermaids from the royal bloodline have been trained as spies to work for the reigning kings and queens, keeping the collection safe from sirens and humans.

Celena and her partner, Merrick, work covertly for the royals—not even her twin brother knows. When they discover the sirens have broken through the barriers the mer set up to keep the sirens out, Celena and her friends must race to the old kingdom of Metten to stop them from starting a war within their borders.

When she's dragged to the surface, Celena realizes that the war above the waters is as deadly as the one below the waves—and sacrificing herself may be the only way to protect her family.

The Siren Wars have only just begun.

Available now!
Learn more about The Siren Wars Saga at sirenwarsinfo.
kmrobinsonbooks.com

**All wishes require sacrifice…*are you willing to
pay the price?***

Cyra spent the last seven years being trained to steal an
airship in a brutal competition that leaves the victor with
millions. Last year, she won.

Aladdin spent the past year fighting to get enough money
to take his mother away from Horallen after his father was
murdered. Now, his evil uncle Kacper wants to force him
into the competition and straight to his death inside the
Collection Cave.

When Aladdin discovers a genie said to have been
banished a century ago, the competition becomes even

deadlier, and he knows he can't trust the girl who snuck into the competition this year…but Cyra might not survive his ruthlessness either in a game where only the lion's heart can win.

All wishes require sacrifice, and someone is going to pay the price for the Stourbridge.

Available now!

Learn more about The Stealing Steam Series at

lionsandlampsinfo.kmrobinsonbooks.com

Little Hacker Muffet
sat on her tuffet
destroying her cords and Way.
Along came a hacker named Spider,
who sat down beside her
and frightened his opponent away.

WHEN FET, ONE OF THE MOST SKILLED HACKERS IN the Legends, discovers her best friend and leader of her group has been abducted and held for ransom, she must escape unnoticed and find Peep before it's too late.

When Spider, a new recruit training to join her hacker ring, slips out with her and claims to have a plan to save her friend, Fet is forced to bring him along. As she discovers he's not who he claims to be, she faces grave danger and learns just how deadly a spider bite can be.

Now available!
Learn more about The Legends Chronicles at
acasinfo.kmrobinsonbooks.com

VIRTUALLY SLEEPING BEAUTY

***T**O WAKE HER UP, HE HAS TO ENTER THE GAME AND help her beat it...*

Surely the class president wouldn't illegally over-juice to stay in the virtual reality game citizens are allowed to play for four hours a day, but when Royce's aunt calls in a panic because her goddaughter hasn't left the game yet, his only option is to go inside the game and drag the girl out.

The golden knight quickly discovers the princess' absence in the real world isn't of her own doing—*she's trapped inside the game by unknown forces*—and if she can't escape soon, she could die for real outside of the game. He's even more shocked to discover that Rora outranks him inside of the game, which means she'll have to fight to *protect herself* from the evils locking her inside a dangerous world.

Can Rora and Royce work together to outsmart a vicious queen and evil magician, and defeat digital dragons, or will Rora slowly fade away until there's nothing left but an empty shell and the game ranking she will leave behind?

Now available!

Learn more about Virtually Sleeping Beauty at
vsbinfo.kmrobinsonbooks.com

THE REVOLUTION OF JACK FROST

No one inside the snow globe knows that Morozoko Industries is controlling their weather, testing them to form a stronger race that can survive the fall out from the bombs being dropped in the outside world—all they know is that they must survive the harsh Winter that lasts a month and use the few days of Spring, Summer, and Fall to gather enough supplies to survive.

When the seasons start shifting, Genesis and Jack know something is going on. As their team begins to find technology that they don't have access to inside their snow globe of a world, it begins to look more and more like one of their own is working against them.

.   .   .

Genesis soon discovers Morozoko Industries, but when a foreign enemy tries to destroy their weather program to make sure their destructive life-altering bombs succeed in destroying the outside world, only one person can shut down the machine that is spinning out of control and save the lives of everyone inside the bunker—Jack.

Now available!
Learn more about The Revolution of Jack Frost at
jackfrostinfo.kmrobinsonbooks.com

Hansel and Gretel's witch was actually on their side...

Annika's job is to create a cake to match the candy-colored rooftops, nightly firework shows, and daily parades ending in unexpected executions for the mad king's ball, but her true mission is to sneak a thirteen-year-old assassin into the palace using her gift of illusions.

Hansel's job is to protect his little sister, Gretel, once she assassinates King Levin and ends the destruction in Candestrachen, using his power over light to rescue the young girl from the chaos her influence over life and death will create.

.   .   .

When the entire forest reconstructs itself under Gretel's command while trying to save herself from a king's guard, Hansel and Annika must put their feelings aside and ensure their plan holds true—even if it means one of them has to sacrifice themselves to protect the mission.

Her illusions were meant to save her....but not everyone will survive the assassination attempt.

Learn more about Sugarcoated at
sugarcoatedinfo.kmrobinsonbooks.com

THE GOOSE GIRL AND THE ARTIFICIAL

What would you do if your artificially intelligent handmaiden stole your identity?

Threatened by her Artificial, Arta, Princess Goselyn is forced to switch places and pretend she isn't human when she reaches Prince Corinth to negotiate a treaty they both need to be able to take their respective crowns one day. If she doesn't comply, her Artificial, controlled by her evil cousin, will not only kill Goselyn's mother, but Prince Corinth and his father as well.

Can the quiet princess outsmart a machine created to be more intelligent than she is, all while surviving the other

Artificials and robots working against her in the foreign palace, or will Corinth and his father find out and destroy her chance to save them all?

Learn more about The Goose Girl and The Artificial at goosegirlinfo.kmrobinsonbooks.com

THE SINKING

The sea witch wants to silence her, but not for the reason you think.

WHEN A QUIRKY OLDER WOMAN PAWNS A FANCY seashell necklace at her mother's antique shop on the pier, Cara doesn't think much about the story the woman spins about the wearer turning into a mermaid.

On her way home, she accidentally drops the necklace into the ocean and is swept out to sea where she meets—a merman who volunteers to take her to his mother, the sea queen, to help her get her legs back.

. . .

Cara soon learns that it's Quay's eighteenth birthday—a day that has been a curse for his family—and is meant to be one for her too. Now she must fight to survive the sea with Quay at her side.

Fans of The Little Mermaid will love this twisted take on the beloved story.

Now available!
Learn more about The Sinking at
thesinkinginfo.kmrobinsonbooks.com

CINDRILL

CINDERELLA IS AN ASSASSIN OUT TO MURDER THE prince...*but he's hunting her too.*

The nanobots Cindrill's master gives her to use as a mask allow her to slip into the ball wearing a face that isn't hers, but when the assassination attempt goes sideways, Prince Davian doesn't understand why her face changes when he injures her, slicing her foot open around a unique pair of shoes as she runs away.

When Cindrill runs into the prince the next day without her nanobot mask on, he doesn't recognize her, but immediately decides her skills will be useful on his hunt for the would-be-assassin woman who nearly killed his father and his fiancée the night before.

Both are tasked with the job of murdering the other, but things don't quite go as they had planned when Cindrill's master and Davian's fiancée interfere as the two try to decide whether or not to kill the other.

It's hard to recognize a woman when she uses technology to change her appearance, but Cindrill is going to use that to her full advantage as she destroys the prince. ***Will either survive?***

Now available!

Learn more about Cindrill at
cindrillinfo.kmrobinsonbooks.com

BLOOD IS SILENT

RED RIDING HOOD IS A CIRCUS AERIALIST AND THE wolf is ready to cage her.

Sienna has grown up working for the circus, dangling off her signature red silks every night. Her grandmother has been known to wander off to train new acts for their boss, but when Sienna tries to find her to bring her back to the show, she doesn't expect the dashing and dangerous Elijah to join her.

When they finally find Grandma Ida has been transformed deep in the heart of the woods, Sienna will stop at nothing to save her—but the wolf has her right where he wants her, and she won't be able to escape his claws.

She was told not to go into the woods alone.

Now available!

Learn more about Blood Is Silent at
bloodissilentinfo.kmrobinsonbooks.com